Tamar will never give up her mother's tapestry....

"How dare you detain me?" The past months of self-reliance had increased Tamar's natural dignity. "Open that door at once or I shall scream and tell everyone here you have insulted me."

His eyelids closed until only a tiny bit of pupil showed. "I wouldn't do that if I were you my dear." He drew himself up. "Your family has worried about you. I feel obligated to report to them your whereabouts." He twisted his lips. "Unless of course you care to make my silence worth my while.... He shrugged.

"You know I have no money," she accused.

"Oh, but you have something infinitely more valuable," he told her. "Lorraine was livid that you clung to an heirloom tapestry she said was worth a fortune."

For a moment, Tamar felt faint. Never in her life had she felt more alone. Yet peace crept into her heart. Hadn't God promised never to forsake her?

COLLEEN L. REECE is a prolific author with over sixty books published including seven Heartsong Presents titles. With the popular Storm Clouds over Chantel, Reece established herself as a doyenne of Christian romance.

Books by Colleen L. Reece

HEARTSONG PRESENTS

HP1—A Torch for Trinity
HP2—Wildflower Harvest
HP7—Candleshine
HP8—Desert Rose
HP16—Silence in the Sage
HP24—Whispers in the Wilderness
HP43—Veiled Joy

ROMANCE READER—TWO BOOKS IN ONE

RR1—Honor Bound & The Calling of Elizabeth Courtland
RR4—To Love and Cherish & Storm Clouds over Chantel
RR6—Angel of the North & Legacy of Silver
RR7—A Girl Called Cricket & The Hills of Hope

Don't miss out on any of our super romances. Write to us at the following address for information on our newest releases and club information.

Heartsong Presents Reader's Service
P.O. Box 719
Uhrichsville, OH 44683

Tapestry of Tamar

Colleen L. Reece

A Sequel to *Veiled Joy*

Heartsong Presents

ISBN 1-55748-443-0

TAPESTRY OF TAMAR

one

Tamar O'Donnell tiptoed to the top step of the gracefully winding staircase. Her Spanish-brown eyes danced. She checked the great hall below, then the halls on either side of her. White teeth gleamed in a smile. Good. Every door stood firmly shut. With a whisper of glee, Tamar gathered up the long black skirts she hated, perched on the shining mahogany banister rail, and pushed off in a slide. She had wanted to do that ever since she came to live with her older brother Carlos in his ornate Nob Hill San Francisco home.

Faster, faster she went, gathering momentum. Carlos's haughty wife Lorraine insisted she wear a black veil to cover her "plebeian red hair," but now it tore free, and Tamar's red-gold curls, inherited from her grandmother Joyous, streamed into confusion.

The massive front door flung open at the same moment Tamar thudded to a stop at the bottom of the staircase. She scrambled to her feet, smoothed down her skirts, and looked up into her sister-in-law's narrow face.

"And what is the meaning of this—this shocking, disrespectful behavior?" Lorraine O'Donnell, not a single hair out of place, glared up at Tamar, whose five foot eight slender height towered over her by a good four inches. Tamar wondered, not for the first time, why Carlos had chosen this cold woman with her correct demeanor and lack of understanding or humor.

"Well?" Lorraine rustled toward her, taffeta petticoats swishing. Her pale green gown did nothing for her blondish hair and grey-green eyes, but it would have changed Tamar from a black specter into a beauty.

Rebellion against the tyranny this woman had shown her crisped Tamar's reply. "Father and Mother never found me shocking or disrespectful. Perhaps because they loved me."

Her shot went home. Angry color suffused Lorraine's carefully guarded pale skin. "Enough of your impertinence, miss. Go to your room."

Tamar clenched her hands into fists behind her black gown. "Don't speak to me as if I were a child." She knew better than to argue with Lorraine but rushed on. "I will be eighteen years old in less than six months."

"Eighteen or eighty, so long as you live in my house you will comport yourself in a ladylike manner, although for you, that appears to be impossible."

"I won't live in your house—which my brother bought, not you—forever." Rage rose within her.

"Bravo!" A young man of middle height, with sleek brown hair and hazel eyes, applauded from the open doorway. "I like my women to show their mettle. Of course, that will have to change if I should decide to marry you." His mocking gaze measured her unbecoming mourning and he shuddered delicately. "Really, Lorraine, must she wear black forever? It makes her look like a red-headed crow and surely offends the sensibilities of anyone with taste who is forced to observed her."

His sarcasm did what Lorraine's order had failed to accomplish. Tears burned Tamar's eyes but her voice was iced as she said, "The day I marry you will be the day I go mad, Phillip-with-two-l's-Carlin." She couldn't resist turning and smiling sweetly after she majestically swept halfway up the stairway. "If Lorraine has indicated otherwise, this is a good time to disabuse you of such ideas."

In the silence that followed she reached the hall above and turned the corner, but halted just out of sight. Instinct told her Lorraine and Phillip would immediately begin discussing her, so Tamar opened the nearest door, slammed it shut, then huddled down on the thick rug and strained her ears to hear the buzz of voices.

"Dear me, I do believe your niece has inherited the temper to go with her hair," Phillip began.

Tamar's lip curled. She could imagine him, leaning against a wall or one of the tall columns that supported the arched roof, too lazy to stand straight. Phillip-with-two-l's, as he perpetually announced himself to strangers, never walked when he could ride, never stood when he could sit. Marrying him would be unbearable. Her heart beat fast when Lorraine's high-pitched voice floated up to her.

"She's young and her parents spoiled her. My husband tried to tell them but they only laughed." Venom filled her voice. "I fought having her come to us when they were killed in that railway accident but Carlos insisted we take her in hand until a suitable match could be arranged. These last six months have been a struggle, I admit. I have seen some improvement but it's 1905, not the eighteen hundreds when young women were glad enough to be sheltered and cared for. I plan to get any modern idea of independence out of Tamar's head, I can tell you that."

The listening girl allowed herself the luxury of a smile but tensed again when Phillip drawled, "I really can't consider her unless I believe I can tame her. Of course, the dowry *is* a consideration."

Tamar didn't have to see him to know how his eyes narrowed with the familiar speculative gleam.

Lorraine's nervous laugh drifted into the upper hall. "You needn't worry about that." She laughed again. "Everyone knows how the O'Donnells struck it rich—them and that old desert rat who found Joyous. The O'Donnell-McFarland holdings at one time were said to contain the most wealth of any property in California or Nevada."

How clever! Disgust gave way to admiration in Tamar's mind. Lorraine hadn't lied; she had simply parroted so-called common knowledge. Tamar started to her feet then paused. Not yet. Not until she heard them out.

"And she will be eighteen in the fall?"

"On October tenth. The terms of her parents' will specifically direct that their leavings be split equally between Carlos, Tamar, and their younger brother Richard—Dick. Tamar will receive her share on her eighteenth birthday."

"The younger brother is in school, isn't he? I wouldn't want to be saddled with a fifteen-year-old if I decide it's worth my while to marry the girl."

"Carlos intends to ship Richard off to West Point once he's old enough," Lorraine quickly assured, while Tamar's fury increased. Wasn't it bad enough to be separated from Dick now that their parents were dead? How would she ever see him if Lorraine forced Carlos to send him even further away?

"Just how much is the inheritance?" His greed added life to Phillip's usually bored voice.

"I'm surprised you ask," Lorraine answered carelessly. "All of San Francisco talks of the fabulous fortune amassed by the O'Donnell's proper investments."

The quiet moments that followed felt like an eternity. Then Phillip said, "My dear Lorraine, October tenth sounds fortuitous for a wedding, don't you think? After the ceremony, your husband can turn Tamar's inheritance over to the proper person to handle it—me."

His smug assurance needled Tamar beyond endurance. She whipped around the corner, scorned the

banister rail, and charged down the staircase toward
the open-mouthed Lorraine and the would-be guard-
ian of her fortune. Enjoyment erased her anger and
she spoke slowly, savoring every word that tore down
Lorraine's carefully constructed plan to get rid of her.

"Dear Phillip." Her voice dripped honey. "My
kind and caring sister-in-law has conveniently forgotten to inform you of something you may find important. Everything she said about the fortune my
ancestors had is true. However, she failed to add that
my father, beloved though he was, didn't inherit the
business sense of his parents and grandparents. He
invested, lost, and in the effort to recoup his losses,
everything was swept away. The train that claimed
my parents' lives was returning from an unsuccessful,
frantic trip Father and Mother took to see if they could
borrow money."

She laughed in sudden gladness at the stupefied
expression on Lorraine's face, the slack-jawed look
Phillip wore. "Did I overhear you making plans for
October tenth?" she wickedly asked. "When dis-
bursement is made, it will be but a pittance, I'm
afraid. Does this make a difference in your inten-
tions?" She bit her lip to keep from laughing.

Phillip finally regained his composure enough to
stiffly say, "This does put a different complexion on
the situation."

What a stuffed owl! Pompous, conceited—Tamar
ran out of adjectives. "Think nothing of it," she told
him. "I wouldn't marry you if San Francisco Bay

swept in and drowned every other man in the city."
She whirled toward Lorraine. "As for you, does
Carlos know your schemes?"

The blonde woman raised a perfect eyebrow. "It
was not I who brought Phillip here. Carlos selected
him a few days after we realized you must live with
us for a time." Every word fell like a cube of ice.
"Phillip, I wouldn't be too concerned about the lack
of a generous dowry. You know I have a personal
fortune in my own right and. . . ." A shrug of her
shoulders filled in the missing words.

So her own brother had been in on the plot. Tamar
took a deep breath. Snobbish and proud she had
known him to be but this? Incredible. Her hurt and
anger blinded her.

She roused when Phillip promised, "We'll speak
more of this when we have the privacy to do so,
Lorraine. For now, *au revoir*." He kissed his
fingertips in the obnoxious way Tamar hated and
waved them at her before vanishing out the front door.

"You expect me to marry that affected person?"
Tamar glared at Lorraine.

"Beggars can't always choose," Lorraine reminded, back in control. She cocked her head to one side
and surveyed Tamar. "Hmm. Phillip is right. I must
speak with Carlos and convince him six months'
mourning is enough. You do look like a red-haired
crow in black." She mounted the stairs of her
mansion, a mansion that looked over—and down
on—the lesser mortals who inhabited San Francisco.

Not until Tamar heard the restrained closing of a door far down the hall above did she break free of the fear that dropped over her like a shroud. Could Carlos and Lorraine force her into a hateful, loveless marriage? She drifted outside into a garden bright with spring flowers that fluttered in the breeze off the bay. A marble fountain, too large for good taste, spattered cool drops against her heated face. If only she could leave this prison on a hill. But where could she go? Dick was too young to help her, and their grandparents had died when Tamar was small. She could barely remember Grandpa Brit's Irish brogue and Grandma Joyous' sparkling blue eyes. Why had her parents and grandparents all died so young, Tamar wondered. Lorraine's comment that it was God's will infuriated her young sister-in-law. How could a loving God, if there were a God at all, take away everyone she needed so desperately?

Tamar sighed. Her parents, Brit Jr. and dark-eyed Rosalind, had believed in God and had taught her to do the same. From early childhood, she had learned how Jesus died to save all those who accepted and served Him. She hadn't questioned—until the train wreck that left her adrift. This new revelation of Carlos's relentless ambition had further shaken her.

If only Uncle Carlos and Aunt Sadie hadn't sailed for Europe just before the accident! Tamar's eyes flashed with golden motes. How different her laughing, handsome uncle was from the nephew who had been named after him. Uncle Carlos was loving and

honest, and he always cared more about people than
he did about money. Tamar had spent hours curled up
on his lap listening to his stories of the rugged Nevada
land and how he, a Monterey dandy, had learned of
life and found love in a rough mining town.

"Your grandfather Brit was the finest man I ever
knew," the older Carlos told Tamar. "Another would
have shipped me out with the first supply wagon for
the crazy things I did." She would never forget the
way he turned to his wife's still-pretty face or the look
he wore when he added softly, "I found out how good
God was and met the only girl in the world for me.
How my proud father raged, until he got to know
Sadie."

But Uncle Carlos and Aunt Sadie were far away
now, too far away to be able to help Tamar. With no
one to appeal to, she accepted the need to outwardly
acquiesce to Lorraine's domination for the next six
months. Inwardly, she would count every day and
plan. The night before her eighteenth birthday, she
mush vanish, no matter what. October tenth would
not be her wedding day to Phillip-with-two-l's. *God*,
her tired heart whispered, *are You here? I need
someone, anyone.* . . . Too perplexed to think more,
Tamar stood and paced the orderly garden paths. She
paused by a date palm and looked out at the blue, blue
sea. She leaned against the palm's rough trunk and
listened to a voice from her childhood.

"Mother, why am I Tamar? Why not Dolores or
Carlotta or Kathleen?" Eyes as dark as Rosalind's

own peered into her mother's face.

"Tamar comes from the Hebrew name that means palm tree. And, little one, a palm tree is a wonderful thing. Sturdy, strong, it sways with the wind but is not broken. It offers comfort to others by giving protection against desert heat. Your grandmother Joyous often spoke of how she treasured the oases with their shade. It was she who named you Tamar Joy O'Donnell. No child could ever have a better name."

Tamar never again complained about her name. And when Lorraine decided she should be known instead as Joyce, Tamar simply refused to respond.

"I don't feel very sturdy or strong," Tamar whispered to a sympathetic flower. "I have to be, though. Somehow I must escape, earn money, and never fail to keep in touch with Dick. He should have been named after Uncle Carlos. Even though Uncle Carlos is really only a distant cousin, Dick looks enough like him to be the son Uncle Carlos and Aunt Sadie never had."

The little respite in the garden gave Tamar strength to endure that evening after dinner while Lorraine told Carlos her version of the afternoon. They sat in the too-fussy, too-crowded expensive parlor that made Tamar feel closed in and unable to breathe. Almost every inch of the walls contained pictures: paintings, family gatherings, revered ancestors. Tamar thought her pictured parents must look down on the clutter with distaste. Their own home had been beautifully but simply furnished. This heavy, dark room bore little resemblance to the airy, spacious rooms where Tamar had romped and studied and grown up.

All through Lorraine's recitation Tamar sat and gazed out the window, passionately wishing she could be free to run. Since arriving on Nob Hill, she had been pronounced too old for such childish behavior. The one time she tried it, Lorraine's wrath had erupted. Since then, Tamar only raced in her thoughts.

"What do you have to say for yourself?" Carlos demanded when the accusations stopped.

"Nothing." She faced him sadly, looking for the love she had always wanted from him. The years had not given him compassion, and his marriage to Lorraine had only worsened his snobbery. Tamar looked for a single glance that told her he understood, some signal of his love, even though she knew he would not cross his wife. No signal came, just a tightening of his fine lips into a straight line.

"There will be no more such incidents." So might a king have dispassionately ordered, "Off with her head."

"No." Tamar knew what she must do. If it took dissembling, so be it. A pretense of giving in would allay suspicion until October ninth. Then she would vanish.

"Very well, you may go."

She started out, wretched at his coldness, glad to be released. His voice stopped her at the door.

"Tomorrow I will talk with Phillip Carlin. If he isn't thoroughly disgusted at the exhibition of temper and low breeding you displayed today, we will announce your betrothal soon."

Tamar wanted to turn, to hurl the truth at him that she'd rather be dead than married to Phillip Carlin. She didn't. Something deep inside warned her that screaming out would lessen her chances for escape. She had six months. If they must be spent as Phillip-with-two-l's fiancee, so be it. But let him touch her and he'd see what a red-headed crow could do!

To the O'Donnell household's amazement, Phillip declined to engage himself to Tamar, maintaining he had been given false information about her fortune. He went even further and intimated that no other eligible young San Francisco bachelor would be any more willing to accept her under the circumstances. Through a series of eavesdroppings, Tamar learned this and covered her mouth with her hands to keep in her glee. But a second, then a third consultation between Carlin and Lorraine ended with a dowry offer from Lorraine large enough to bring Carlin to agreement. Tamar, watching from the shelter of a large shrub in the garden, could have told Lorraine and Carlos why Carlin gave in to the engagement. A parlor maid who liked the homeless girl had pursed her lips when Tamar first asked her what she knew about Phillip Carlin, but later she unzipped them. Carlin's own fortunes were none too secure, the maid told Tamar. His gambling and love for luxury combined with his equal hate for work, even to the point that he refused to be bothered by checking up on those he hired to manage his business interests. The result was near financial disaster, although he kept the secret.

"I know 'tis true," the parlor maid hissed. "My sister's been keepin' company with Carlin's man and he told her."

One good thing that came from the betrothal was Carlos's permission to discard mourning. Under Lorraine's supervision, the best dressmaker in San Francisco undertook a complete wardrobe for Tamar. Wise in her craft and with an eye to the monetary gains promised, she wisely placated Lorraine, while relying almost solely on Tamar's instinct for clothes. She bypassed style if it did not enhance Tamar's bright hair, white skin, and near-black eyes. "You aren't beautiful," the dressmaker told her. "But you're striking and that's better." Soft blues and greens, pale apricot and peach gowns lined Tamar's clothes rack. White—often touched with a single accent of ruby, sapphire, emerald—but no pink or red. Dark colors only for riding and then brightened with the incomparable touches of a couturier.

Out of mourning, accompanied by Phillip, Tamar's love of opera and drama lightened her spirits. No one was more sought after for soirees and teas, receptions and balls. Visiting dignitaries who expected boredom, lost their ennui when Tamar sang. In fact she often put to shame those who appeared in the various opera halls. Untrained though her voice was, it held the sweetness of youth and the clarity of a sun-filled

sky. Even Phillip gradually put aside his disdain and
swelled with pride when his fiancee captured hearts
with her voice.

Yet as days fled into weeks, weeks into months,
Tamar grew weary of trying to plan her escape.
Sometimes she wondered if she might better just give
in and become Mrs. Phillip Carlin. Her choices
offered little other hope. She could not earn her living
at sewing or nursing, she drearily thought. What else
was there for a respectable girl? She often wondered
why God hadn't allowed her to be on the train with her
parents when they had died.

two

August sped like a racing horse. Tamar wondered how the days and nights could go so rapidly. Her periods of rebelliousness dwindled into a dull acceptance of the life Carlos and Lorraine had laid out for her. Ironically, her occasional spurts of rebellion often followed her fiancé's repeated, "Phillip-with-two-l's" pretensions.

"Why do you insist on saying that?" Tamar blurted out one day as, against Phillip's wishes, they waited for a cable car. He scorned public transportation and preferred to be driven by private conveyance. Today, though, Tamar had expressed a desire to go by cable car as a change.

"My dear girl." His patronizing air set her teeth on edge. "If one doesn't value oneself and insist that others do so, one will never be taken at one's full value."

"You sound like a paragraph from *The Book of Manners*," she muttered.

He shrugged in the way she particularly detested. "I do have the experience and wisdom of a man five years older than you," he silkily reminded her. "You must learn not to question me."

Tamar set her lips in a firm line and subsided.

Picking an argument with Phillip was as useless as arguing with the tall bedposts in her ornate room. She changed tactics. "After we're mar-married—" She stumbled over the word. "Where will we live? Can we have a house of our own?"

He raised his eyebrows in distaste. "What common tastes you have. With the rather generous dowry you bring me we will be able to live in one of the finer hotels, at least for a time." He smoothed his sleek brown hair back over his forehead. His well-cared for hand had probably never done anything much more strenuous then lift a glass of fine liqueur.

The thought made Tamar's lips twitch but she asked curiously, "Haven't you ever wanted to do something with your life, Phillip? Most men, even rich ones, have duties. You never seem to."

"Why should I?" He sounded genuinely surprised and his hazel eyes opened wider than usual. "That's what managers and investments brokers and servants are for."

"And if they don't serve you well?" Tamar thought of the gossip passed on by the parlor maid.

He laughed uneasily. "Don't brother your pretty head about such matters. Things have a way of straightening themselves out."

She silently gazed out over the bay, noting the whitecaps that rose and fell with the gathering wind. Such an attitude opposed everything Tamar believed. Her father had lost everything because of a careless attitude toward his possessions.

Of course Carlos and Lorraine also lived lavishly. Carlos had been shrewd enough to take the money given to him on his twenty-first birthday, invest, and reap returns. Buying up land that once lay worthless, Carols convinced businessmen to purchase it and expand with the growing city. He also kept several choice parcels on which important buildings stood and from these he collected rich rentals. Yet time after time Tamar had heard her brother and his wife "talking poor mouth," as Tamar privately called it, as if they were already knocking on the door of the poorhouse. Was there security anywhere?

Once she had felt secure because of her parents and God. The long months after their death had shaken her faith in Him, even more violently than the quakes that shook the city.

She thought of the sharp earthquakes that set the chandeliers to chattering and rattled windows. Perhaps the city should have paid the Japanese scientist Mr. Omori the two thousand dollars he asked for an instrument to predict quakes. But most people only laughed and shrugged off the shakes as inevitable and harmless. After all, they told themselves, less deaths had been recorded from earthquakes than from carriage accidents.

Others reassured themselves by remembering how the Indians of the area laughed at the Spaniards' fears when Yerba Buena, later renamed San Francisco, was established in the spring of 1776. The Indians said that yes, the earth shivered, but it did no harm. After all, the Indians had always lived there. Yet sometimes when the ground trembled beneath Tamar's feet, her heart leaped with fear.

"I've spoken to you three times." Phillip's petulant voice recalled her to the present. Tamar felt as if she had come back from a long journey. A journey—the word combined with the sight of the white wake of a distant ship to generate a wild scheme. What if she stowed away? She had heard of boys doing that. She could cut her hair, don boys' clothing and. . . . The plan died a-borning. Phillip-with-two-l's might be overbearing but she would be safer with him than aboard a ship. Yet how could she marry a man she didn't respect, let alone love? She sighed.

"You wanted to ride the cable car. The least you can do is act as if you're enjoying it," Phillip told her.

She forced a trembling smile, but her mind churned. Somehow, in some way, she must come up with a plan to escape.

Suddenly, September marked the end of summer, although flowers bloomed just as brightly and the warm sun poured over the city by the bay. With every passing day, Tamar withdrew more into herself. She refused to rise to Lorraine's baiting, silently reproached Carlos with her dark eyes, and gave up trying to find any ambition in Phillip. Not until Lorraine announced the October tenth wedding would outshine the finest ever held in San Francisco, did Tamar demur.

"Isn't it bad enough to be sold on the auction block

like a slave, without forcing me to pretend to like it?" she demanded, her face white with anger.

"Would you like it better if we asked Phillip to sneak away to some obscure place and marry you?" Lorraine's narrow face set into an unpleasant mask. "He and we have a position to uphold. It's going to be bad enough when Nob Hill learns the pitiful state of your parents' holdings."

"Why is it any of their concern?" Tamar didn't back down. Heartsick and desperate, she knew this might be her last protest. After October tenth, never again would she be able to call her soul her own. She would be Phillip's possession, bought and paid for with his position in society. Her mouth twisted. If precious Nob Hill knew what a sham Phillip Carlin really was, they would draw aside in horror. But Lorraine's rigid posture showed the futility of argument. Tamar left her muttering comments about the ungratefulness of those who should be thankful for their daily bread.

Tamar stood passively for endless fittings, noting the gleam of approval Lorraine couldn't hide. Had her sister-in-law always been the same—gloating over what she owned? Tamar could envision Lorraine as a child dressing an exquisite doll in French silk and satin, then displaying it to others with the same gloating pleasure she now showed. Tamar might just as well have been one more of Lorraine's lovely possessions, for without conceit, the reluctant bride recognized her own attractiveness. She would far rather have been old and ugly; then perhaps Phillip wouldn't have considered her, no matter how large her dowry.

October storms blew in, no wilder than Tamar's despair. Weeks of waiting melted into days. She had considered and rejected hundreds of escapes and at last admitted there was no way out. The God of her childhood had forgotten her or long before now He would have answered when she pounded on heaven's gates to be heard. Yet a tiny spark persisted and no amount of reason could drown it totally. It took a last, heartrending incident to fan the spark into a conflagration.

Two days before the wedding date, Tamar trudged up the beautiful staircase to the borrowed sanctuary her room had become. She gasped when she stepped through the open door. "What is the meaning of this?"

The parlor maid stopped her work and sent a pitying glance at the white-faced girl. Tamar ran to the shelves where she had kept her treasures, few in number but infinitely precious. A senorita doll named Rosa. The few "suitable" books Lorraine had allowed her to keep from her parents' great library. A Mexican tapestry. "Where are they, my things?"

"The madam ordered them to be taken away." Resentment and compassion tinged the colorless voice, and the parlor maid pointed to an old sack. Rosa sat sprawled among the books, one arm up as though warding off a death blow. The gorgeous tapestry, woven in the red, green, and white national colors of Mexico, lay crumpled on the floor next to the sack.

At that moment, Tamar knew she would never again live under the tyranny of brother, sister-in-law, or husband. She snatched the generous length of tapestry, the only thing she had from her mother, and held it close to her.

The parlor maid furtively slipped to the door and closed it. Her pale eyes shone and she lowered her voice to a whisper. "Miss Tamar, if you like, I'll hide the books and doll in my room. You'll want to take the tapestry with you, I'm sure."

"You'll be in trouble if Lorraine finds out," Tamar protested. Her fingers tightened on the tapestry.

"The madam's not likely to be poking under a parlor maid's bed, 'specially when it's in a dim attic." The woman quickly grabbed the sack, straightened the books and laid Rosa on top. She opened the door, put her finger to her lips, and slipped through. Tamar's heart pounded, but when Lorraine stepped inside a few minutes later and surveyed the room, Tamar flared at her. "You had no right." She still clutched the tapestry.

"I have every right in my own house," Lorraine reminded. "Give me that dirty old rag."

"It's not a dirty rag and you know it. This tapestry is generations old and worth a great deal of money." Tamar wished she'd held her tongue. Avarice filled Lorraine's watching eyes.

"Then it should be sold immediately." She held out

her hand. "After all, you owe me for your dowry."

All the heartache and misery Tamar had built up for the past year flooded through her. "Never!" She struck down the reaching hand, flung the tapestry over her head, and raced out.

"Tamar Joyce O'Donnell, come back here this instant!"

She heard Lorraine's quick footsteps behind her. They only spurred her on. Down, down she ran. Whatever lay on the other side of the heavy front door couldn't be worse than—

She careened full speed into Carlos.

"Let me go," she panted, struggling against his iron grip.

"Have you gone mad?" His icy composure didn't keep him from pinioning her arms and preventing escape. "Lorraine, for the love of heaven, what brought this on?'

Face livid, hand red where Tamar had struck it, she reached the bottom of the stairs. "Look at what this— wildcat did!" She held out her shaking hand. "All because of *that*." She pointed toward the tapestry that had slid from Tamar's head to her shoulders.

"She took it away, everything I love!" Tamar cried. "Rosa. My books. She ordered them taken away and destroyed."

Shock loosened Carlos's grip for an instant and his sister pulled free. Hope surged through her, even though he still blocked her path to the door and freedom. "Lorraine!" He stared at his wife. "That tapestry is almost priceless."

"Then let it be sold so your beggar of a sister can help repay some of the dowry we are giving," she snapped.

"Tamar is not a beggar and the tapestry is hers." His cold tones matched her own.

"Does it excuse her striking your wife?" Lorraine played her best card.

"Tamar, did you hit her?" Understanding vanished in rage.

Words of defense rushed to her lips and died there.

"See, she cannot deny it because it's true." Lorraine rubbed her hand. "I suggest locking her in her room until the wedding—unless you want a missing bride."

"All this fuss over nothing." Carlos gritted his teeth and cast a gaze heavenward. "Tamar, you will go to your room and remain there. Your meals will be served to you and a servant will watch outside your locked door. Never have I been so glad for a wedding to take place. Don't think Phillip won't deal with you if you behave in such a reprehensible way once you're his."

She mentally measured the distance to the front door, considered fleeing into the dining room and out through the kitchen, and thought better of it. Her last hope lay in passiveness. She turned and slowly mounted the staircase, making sure her shoulders slumped in pretended defeat.

"You shouldn't have taken the child's treasures." Carlos's low voice reached her when she had performed her little trick of door slamming, then crouching on the rug just around the corner of the upper hall.

"Taking her part is inexcusable," Lorraine's voice was coming closer. The listener stood and stole to her room. Once inside her prison, she locked the door herself. Her sister-in-law rattled the door and called, but Tamar did not open it. Not until the parlor maid knocked and said she had a dinner tray did Tamar budge from the bed where she'd thrown herself. She started to say she wasn't hungry and would never eat another bite in Carlos's house, but she decided that would only make things worse. Besides, what little money she had been able to hoard wouldn't take her far. Better to stuff herself and hope it wouldn't choke her.

After the first few bites it got easier. Even grief and fear couldn't compete with a healthy young appetite. Tray emptied, she settled down to think. Day after tomorrow she would be eighteen—and married if she didn't get away. It must not happen. She crept to the window and looked out. What a long way down! She shivered. At least the second-story windows were not barred like the lower ones. Would the sturdy vines hold her and offer footholds? *God, this is it. You'd better help me when I climb out this window—or I'll break a leg.* She stifled a giggle. A broken leg would post-pone the wedding but not cancel it.

While Carlos and Lorraine slept, Tamar tore and knotted her sheets into the semblance of a rope, coolly planning her departure. Tomorrow she would act as normal as a jailed criminal could. She would never tell Lorraine she was sorry for striking her, though. Tamar hated a liar. Sometime after midnight of the next evening, she'd go—where? She refused to think about it. Time enough for that once she got away from Lorraine and Carlos. Besides, being eighteen should make a difference, for at last she would be entitled to her small inheritance.

In the long, dark hours, she prayed for fog the following night and rejoiced when she awakened from an uneasy sleep to find a soft, grey day instead of the sunny weather they'd been having. Perhaps God had heard her after all.

When night finally came, her love of pretty dresses caused her to first don a crisp pale green voile before putting on the black. She stuffed underclothing and stockings into a large, striped, woven Mexican bag with the tapestry hidden at the very bottom. She still had room for a long dark skirt and a plain white waist. Finished with her meager packing, Tamar sat in a chair by the window until the toll of the harbor bell and the twelve strikes of a hall clock announced a new day—her eighteenth birthday.

Trembling fingers slid the long bed sheet rope through the bag's handle. She gently lowered the bag and gasped when it swung against the house with a gentle thud. She waited, holding her breath. When the silence continued, she let down the rope and released one end. The heavily packed bag fell the rest of the way and landed in a clump of bushes. Again she held her breath. Surely someone must have heard the solid thump when it hit!

"Thank You, God," she whispered a few moments later. With a backwards glance at the room, Tamar flung a heavy black shawl over her shoulders. Her lightning check of the room showed the heavy chest of drawers she had moved inch by cautious inch from its usual spot to block the door. Her rope was knotted securely around a bed-post.

A pang of regret filled her. Not for leaving this house but for the loving abode her brother's home should have been. A moonbeam pierced the fog just long enough to show the floating white wedding dress ready for the morrow and a bride who would never wear it. What if Phillip had been a different kind of man, one she loved and trusted? A man who loved his Lord and her? Instead of endangering her life by escaping out a window, she would be peacefully sleeping now, or joyously lying awake anticipating a new life.

Close to tears, she put aside such thoughts. She needed all her concentration to do what she must. She swung one booted foot out the window to test the rope. It held. Slowly, more frightened than she'd been since they told her of the train wreck that took her parents' lives, Tamar descended. At last, after what seemed like hours, she dangled a few feet above the ground. Just below lay the bush that held her possessions. Out from it, smooth lawn wet with mist offered a safe landing. She pushed off with her feet, waited until she swung out from the house, and let go. The grass welcomed her with its coolness but she scrambled to her feet. If she were discovered now, nothing on earth could save her from tomorrow's judgment.

In an agony of fear, Tamar retrieved her bag, pulled her shawl close against the chilly night, and lightly ran across the lawn and through the gate. Her shawl and a black veil, the same veil she had once vowed never to wear again, gave her protection, as did the drifting fog.

Night-blooming flowers scented the still air and the mournful sound of a bell buoy filled her ears. Her shoulders straight, just-eighteen-year-old Tamar O'Donnell walked away into the San Francisco fog. She wondered if life would always be gray.

three

Disturbed by the scene with Tamar, Carlos slept fitfully, haunted by his dead mother's accusing gaze. He started up several times, perspiring in spite of the chill night, then thrashed about until Lorraine sleepily demanded, "Whatever is wrong with you? How's a person to get any rest with you groaning and tossing?"

He didn't answer but slid from the massive, antique bed and into a dressing gown. The clock in the hall chimed two. Not since the night he learned his parents had been killed in the train wreck had Carlos been filled with the foreboding that now drove him to his fine library. He paced for a good hour and at last lay down on a settee and fell asleep, to dream again. Confound that girl, Carlos thought when he woke for the dozenth time. Confound Lorraine, too. Why did she have to shove all this folderol on Tamar? He wondered why he had married Lorraine, with her exaggerated idea of her own importance. A streak of inherent honesty forced him to admit he had been as much attracted to her secure finances as to her proud, cold beauty.

Never had dawn been more welcome than on his sister's birthday and wedding day. He peered into the murky world, sighed, and hoped the fog would lift to produce a glorious October day. "If we can just get through without another tantrum," Carlos muttered. He refused to identify whether the tantrums belonged to sister or wife.

"Tamar's evidently still sulking in her room," Lorraine announced as she unfolded her breakfast napkin and attacked chilled grapefruit segments. Even this early, every hair lay in place, sculptured until she looked more like a mannequin than a wife. "I tapped and told her not to be late for breakfast but she refused to answer." Without waiting for a response, she sipped her coffee, then sharply struck a small silver bell. A tired-faced maid came and Lorraine waved at the cup. "Take it away and bring fresh. This tastes like the cook made it from bay water."

Carlos caught the maid's resentful look but he only shrugged. Servants might not like serving the O'Donnells, but they usually stayed because of the good wages. He laid his heavy silver fork across his plate. "Let her sleep. After today you—we won't have to worry about her."

"Poor Phillip. I pity him. On the other hand, I'm sure he can control Tamar."

Why should the memory of the girl's reproachful dark gaze rise between Carlos and his breakfast? Carlos concentrated on the perfectly boned fish on a nest of parsley, flanked with hot buttered biscuits. "He had better. It is costing us plenty."

"You mean it is costing me." Lorraine never passed up an opportunity to remind Carlos she had brought more worldly goods to their marriage than her husband, despite his shrewd dealing. "It will be worth it. By the way, just how much *is* there left from your parents' estate for Tamar?"

"Not much." Carlos squirmed. "By rights, whatever my parents left should go strictly to Tamar and Richard. When Father and Mother made their will, they had no reason to suspect an early demise. If they had lived and Father hadn't lost his money, Tamar and Richard would each have received the same amount on their twenty-first birthday that I did."

"Horrors, they won't make a fuss, will they?" Lorraine dropped her spoon with a little crash. Her gray-green eyes turned flinty.

"It would do no good if they did. The money is no longer there." A frown puckered his heavy dark eyebrows. "I am considering giving my share of the inheritance as a wedding present."

"That is the stupidest remark I have ever had the misfortune to hear," Lorraine flared. "The dowry Phillip insisted on is more than enough wedding gift." She added, "That tapestry should have been sold, as well."

"The tapestry will never go out of the O'Donnell family." He flung down his napkin and rose; all the proud ancestry that ruled his life rose with him. "I'll hear no more about it." He strode off with his wife temporarily silenced. Not often did Carlos take a strong stand. When he did, fighting his will was like trying to turn the tide. Now he turned when he reached the doorway. "Remember, let Tamar sleep. The wedding isn't until this evening and we don't want a washed-out bride." His footsteps echoed down the polished hall.

Lorraine brooded all morning but held her peace. Just a few more hours and they would be rid of Tamar. Even when the parlor maid informed her that Tamar hadn't touched her breakfast tray, Lorraine merely nodded and said nothing, although she gritted her teeth against the hot anger inside. She went upstairs to calm herself by gloating over her own costume, carefully chosen to set off her cool loveliness.

She didn't known an unexpected caller had come until Carlos sent a servant to request her presence in the library immediately. She patted her hair into place, smoothed a bit of lace on her gown, and sauntered downstairs into the dark, oppressive room.

"I'm terribly sorry, but I don't see how I can be held accountable." The family solicitor wrung his hands in distress. "She brought the proof and I—"

"You doddering old fool!" Carlos raised his hand, and for a moment, Lorraine thought he would strike the white-haired lawyer.

"Mr. O'Donnell, you forget yourself." Her rapier voice sliced the tension in the room. "What is this all about?"

Carlos ran a finger under his collar as if it choked him. "This—*donkey* has made a fool of himself and us."

Lorraine gave her distraught husband a scornful

glance and turned to the solicitor. "Speak. What has upset my husband?"

Reassured by her manner, the man told his story. "I arrived late at my office and found my junior partner had taken things into his own hands. But she did bring her papers and he had no way of knowing—"

"*Knowing what?*" If he didn't make sense soon Lorraine felt she would shriek.

Carlos clutched her arm with a steel-band grip. "Tamar waltzed into the office this morning, showed proof she was eighteen today, and convinced this idiot's helper she was entitled to receive her share of our inheritance."

"Wha-at!" Lorraine's jaw dropped. "Impossible! She is locked in her room." She jerked free and started for the door, then whirled. "Are you *sure* the person who carried the papers wasn't an impostor?"

The old man shook his head. "My partner has known Tamar O'Donnell for years."

"But she's being married this evening," Lorraine protested. "The distribution of her inheritance was to be after the ceremony."

"I know." The solicitor's forehead creased with fresh worry. "My partner reported that when he said he understood this was the plan, she stared through him and retorted, 'There will be no wedding. I am eighteen, the money is mine, and I suggest you speedily produce it.' She flustered him so much that he gave her a draft for the money. Whereupon, she bowed and left."

Speechless, the O'Donnells stared at him as he continued. "As soon as I came in, he told me of the curious incident. I sent him posthaste to the bank to see if the draft had been cashed."

"And?" Carlos' eyelids narrowed to slits.

"It had already been cashed." The solicitor mopped his brow. "I'm terribly sorry, as I said, but after all the young woman was legally entitled—"

"Get out." The words fell like two stones.

The old man gathered the remnants of his dignity and escaped. The moment he left the house, Carlos and Lorraine hurried upstairs.

"I still think it was an impostor," Lorraine panted.

"Then you're as big a fool as the one who just left." Carlos knew his sister was gone, but still he thundered through the door, "Tamar, unlock this door and come out here immediately." Silence. He shouted again, heedless of the bevy of curious servants. When he still received no response, he demanded a key, unlocked the door, and gave it a mighty shove. It only opened a few inches.

"What on earth?" Carlos threw his full weight against the solid door. This time he managed to budge the heavy chest of drawers his resourceful younger sister had put there for a barricade. He stepped into the room. The smooth, unwrinkled bed, a crude rope of knotted bed-sheets hanging out the open window, and the desolation of emptiness mutely told their story.

Lorraine regained control first. "Not a word of this

or every one of you will be fired and given no recommendations," she told the cowering staff. "Go." One by one they slipped away, but not before Lorraine caught the little smile on the parlor maid's face, gone so quickly Lorraine couldn't be sure what it had meant.

"Dios!" It was the closest thing to prayer Carlos had uttered for years. He hastened to the window, saw the broken shrubs below. Unwilling admiration crept into his eyes, but anger soon replaced it. He turned on his heel.

"You did this," he accused his wife. "If you had been more understanding, she wouldn't have left."

"I!" Lorraine O'Donnell drew herself to her full height. "You blame me for that vixen's actions?" They rapidly progressed into a quarrel that left Carlos cursing and his wife livid. At last Lorraine whimpered, "We have to find her, bring her back. If she doesn't marry Phillip as planned, what will people *say*?"

"We'll have to tell him." Carlos sat down heavily, faced with disgrace in the eyes of Nob Hill.

"We could say nothing. This may simply be a final prank to annoy us," Lorraine offered. Her face showed she didn't believe a word of her explanation, but she went on anyway, as though trying to convince herself. "It would be just like her to appear any time, smile and go on with the wedding. In the meantime, don't you know someone who could look for her? Someone who could keep his mouth shut?"

Carlos sat with his shoulders slumped. He seemed to barely hear her. "There isn't another man, is there? Someone she cares about and would go to?"

"Don't be ridiculous. When have I allowed her to be anywhere except with Phillip?" Lorraine's reasonable answer set Carlos free from that doubt.

At the end of the day, Carlos and Lorraine had no more idea where Tamar had gone than when they first discovered her to be missing. A grilling interview with the solicitor's junior partner disclosed only that she had been wearing "something light greenish, fluffy-looking" and Lorraine identified it as Tamar's new voile gown. Beyond that, Tamar might as well have walked directly from the law office into the deep blue water of San Francisco Bay.

Afterward, Carlos wondered how he could have let Lorraine convince him to remain silent for so long. She insisted on going to the church, as though the wedding ceremony would still take place. "Tamar may just show up," she excused herself. A few at a time, then dozens and hundreds of guests arrived and were seated. The organ began to play. If anyone wondered why the groom and his attendants appeared rather tardily, well, wedding participants often lagged.

Carlos and Lorraine remained in an anteroom until time for the "mother of the bride" to be seated. Phillip still had not been told anything except that Tamar would be a little late. A dull ache in Carlos's chest spread throughout his whole body as he peered into the growing dusk, hoping to see some conveyance bringing Tamar. The same accusations he'd heard in his dreams now rose in his mind and convicted him. Did his little sister dread marriage with Phillip so much she would actually leave him at the altar? Why hadn't he seen it? Why had he allowed Lorraine to quell his doubts with an airy, "All girls feel nervous and jittery. Once they're married, things will be fine."

No one had thought to tell the organist of the delay. Following his instructions, he went through his repertoire, peered down and saw Lorraine in her place, and joyously burst into the familiar opening of "The Wedding March." Six bridesmaids, chosen from the city's elite, marched to the front. Heads turned in anticipation. Someone stood and the rest of the guests followed. The music went on. And on. Yet the aisle decked in white velvet remained empty. Phillip's lips set in a line that harbored no good for the absent bride. Still the organ pealed and chimed its welcome, until even the hired musician realized something must be amiss. At last he throttled to a stop, with only a weird echo to disturb the waiting silence.

Ashen-faced, finally accepting the truth that Tamar had not and would not come, Carlos took the hardest step of his life and walked slowly down the long aisle alone, the aisle where Tamar should have paced with him. He reached the front, turned, and said quietly but in a tone every listening ear could hear, "I am sorry but my sister is—not well. Thank you for coming." He glanced at Phillip and watched him quickly hide his consternation beneath his pride, and then Carlos turned to help Lorraine to her feet. They marched out to a buzzing recessional of shock, the bridesmaids' pastel gowns fluttering behind them. Would Tamar be hiding in her room at home?

Common sense told Carlos no. In a flash of memory, he recalled the story of Grandmother Joyous, who once fled from an elite family who wanted no part of her. Tamar, a throwback to that brave woman, had not only her grandmother's red-gold hair but also her valor. She would not return so quickly. How long could she live on the paltry inheritance she had collected this morning? What would she do then? Had any man ever been more plagued than Carlos O'Donnell?

An hour later, all of Nob Hill whispered of the wedding that wasn't. Veronica Rhys, who lived with her younger brother Gordon, flounced down on the sofa of their tasteful home not far from the O'Donnells' and prepared to enlighten him about the fiasco. Her ice-blue gown made a pretty splash of color against the dark red upholstery.

"Well, I just wasted an evening," she began. Thirty-nine, as sandy-haired and gray-eyed as thirty-year-old Gordon, their Welsh ancestry showed in more than their name. Yet the stockiness that made Gordon's five foot ten, one hundred and eighty pound frame attractive only made Veronica square and imposing. Despite her lack of beauty, she lived with the conviction that while God might rule the world, she was a divinely appointed second-in-command. Her self assurance was the only quality she shared with Lorraine O'Donnell—whom she secretly despised.

Gordon looked up from some papers he had been scanning. He wore a sympathetic smile. Overbearing, Puritanistic, and annoying as Veronica could be, he adored her. When their mother had died, Veronica had cared for Gordon herself, though she was barely in her teens. "That's too bad. What happened? Oh, yes—the Carlin wedding." He grinned. "Did Phillip duck out? It would be just like him."

Veronica shook her head and a faint twinkle made her less formidable and more human. "No, but the girl did."

Gordon dropped his pen, all attention. "What! You mean any girl or woman in San Francisco would dare leave Carlin at the altar?"

"Carlos O'Donnell explained that his sister was not well but I have my doubts about that." She looked smug. "I don't know Miss O'Donnell but according to her sister-in-law Lorraine she's a redheaded vixen who won't be told anything. Perhaps she got wind of how deeply in debt Phillip really is."

Gordon lost interest. "She should thank God she isn't married to Carlin. He has a long way to go before he will ever become a husband for any decent woman." He smiled at Veronica. "I'd better finish my work. Thanks for the news."

She rose, patted his shoulder. "Goodnight, Gordon."

"Goodnight, Veronica." He watched her leave the room, admiring her stately carriage. Why hadn't some man snatched her up years before? He laughed out loud. For that matter, why hadn't he found a mate among their hordes of friends? His laugh died. Well-meaning associates often accused the Rhys brother and sister of being so compatible they'd never marry.

"Hogwash." The epithet sounded foreign to the elegant room, but Gordon didn't care. Tired of the preparation for the next day's court cases, he thrust back from his desk and strode to the window. Who would have dreamed that one day he and Veronica would live on Nob Hill? He thought of his years as a struggling attorney, how his sister schemed and worked to bring him to the attention of a fine firm. True, the inheritance from their parents had helped. But Veronica's shrewd business sense added to it. Now, without conceit, Gordon knew himself to be one of the most sought after lawyers in the city.

On top of the world, he thought. Yet— He sighed. The talk of the wedding had stirred something deep within him. He was in a position now to look around for a wife, but he felt a strange reluctance. The women he met left him cold with their simpering and their greedy interest in an eligible lawyer bachelor. "Red-headed vixen, eh. At least this Miss O'Donnell sounds like she has brains enough to think, which is more than most society belles do! Wonder if she is sick? Or just stubborn?" He eyed his cluttered desk with distaste, but he gave in to the discipline ingrained in him by a life of hard work. Five minutes later, legal work replaced Carlin and the O'Donnells in his mind. By the next day, he had forgotten his fleeting interest in the "redheaded vixen."

Gordon successfully defended his client, felt the glow that came when he knew justice had been served, then hurried back to his office. A hasty sandwich, coffee, and he plunged back into his work.

"Mr. Rhys, there is a gentleman here to see you," his secretary announced, interrupting his concentration.

"Does he have an appointment, Hood?'

The pallid young man, whose weak face disguised a sharp mind, grimaced. "Carlos O'Donnell considers himself above needing appointments."

"Tell him I only see people with appointments. No, wait." O'Donnell. Red-headed vixen. Could this be. . .? "On second thought, is he the O'Donnell whose sister didn't marry Phillip Carlin last night?"

"The same." Pale he might be, but the secretary kept his finger on the pulse of San Francisco society and had proved himself invaluable.

"I think I'll see him after all." Gordon turned his gaze to the doorway. Since he would never defend a client unless he was convinced of the person's innocence, he had trained himself to make accurate first assessments. Now his keen eyes noticed the arrogance of the faultlessly garbed man who stepped into his office. For a moment Gordon regretted breaking the no-appointment rule. A second later, however, he was convinced that his first instincts had been right after all. Proud, haughty, Carlos O'Donnell stood before him as one who is used to having his own way. Yet the suffering in his dark eyes attested to a sleepless night.

"Mr. Rhys, I need your help," he said simply. "My sister has disappeared." Carlos struggled for control. His voice lowered until Gordon had to lean forward to hear him. "I'm horribly afraid something will happen to her and it will be my fault."

four

Honest and true himself, Gordon Rhys admired a man who could admit and accept the blame for his own actions. Gordon's hand shot across his desk, gripped Carlos O'Donnell's, and shook it heartily. "Have a seat, sir, and let's hear the story. My sister Veronica mentioned there had been a—hitch in the wedding."

Carlos laughed bitterly. "The hitch is that Tamar turned eighteen yesterday, escaped from her locked room by way of a bed sheet rope, and marched into our family solicitor's office with the bit between her teeth. According to the senior attorney, his junior partner found himself squelched by Tamar's manner. So much so that he gave her a draft for her share of our parents' inheritance."

Gordon's eyes glowed. "At least she has spunk."

"Spunk!" Carlos exploded. "She's a twentieth-century replica of our grandmother, red-gold hair, daring, temper, and all." Anger gave way to worry and two sharp vertical lines creased his smooth forehead. "I knew she was against marrying Carlin, but—"

"Any decent woman would be," Gordon interjected.

Carlos shrugged. "Phillip has lived the life of a

bachelor."

"But not all bachelors live the life Phillip has," the young attorney crisply reminded.

Carlos ignored that truth. "The important thing is to find and bring Tamar back, before Nob Hill rocks with news of her flight."

Sympathy warred with distaste, and Gordon shoved his chair back until it squeaked in protest. "Mr. O'Donnell, you must understand something. I won't be able to help you if you plan to coerce your sister into marrying Carlin, should we find her."

Carlos leaped as if stung. His eyes looked like glowing coals in his face. "What business is it of yours what happens after she is found?"

"You made it my business when you walked through my door unannounced," Gordon told him.

Unwilling admiration crept into Carlos' eyes. "What are you, the champion of fair womanhood, a modern Sir Lancelot?"

Gordon threw back his head and laughed. "Far from it. I just can't in good conscience take your case if it means that after your sister's glorious defiance of Carlin, she's still to be sacrificed. Man, can't you imagine how he will treat her? No one of my acquaintance resents a slur more than Phillip. He will never forgive her, even if she marries him."

Carlos spread his hands eloquently. "What other choice have I? My wife is enraged and predicts we will be ostracized when this scandal leaks out."

"Better that than a worse scandal when your young

sister discovers the depths of Carlin's hidden life. She'd be certain to leave him."

"I never considered that. I'm sure Lorraine hasn't, either." Carlos remained silent for a few moments, then frowned and said, "I *must* find Tamar. She's my sister and I love her, though I may not have shown it in the proper way."

Gordon was glad to be saved from the necessity of a reply when O'Donnell added, "Mr. Rhys, I can promise you that if you find Tamar and bring her home, I will not force her into a loveless marriage." Sincerity rang in his voice and Gordon found himself again liking the man. His Spanish heritage of pride had been knifed by his sister's disappearance, but his practical Irish side recognized his own part in the messy business.

"In that case, I can promise you we will do everything possible to locate your sister's whereabouts." Out of curiosity, Gordon asked, "Why is it you came to me rather than your own solicitors?"

Carlos laughed and the genuine mirth cleared the air as nothing else could have done. Gordon found himself wondering if the sister possessed the same charm. "Frankly, Mr. Rhys," Carlos said, "I said some rather rash things to my solicitor. I doubt that just now he will be feeling kindly toward me." The laughter left his face. "I can't take the chance that any investigation he started would be without real interest. I need a man who will care about the outcome of this case. I've heard you only take cases you believe in." His shrewd gaze bored into Gordon. "You proved that when you extracted the condition from me before accepting my case."

What a strange combination of hauteur, genuine warmth, and astuteness! O'Donnell had obviously had a bad shock, one that had shaken him more than the San Francisco tremors that plagued the city. Gordon reached for pen and paper. "Now, tell me every detail, give me the name and address of your sister's friends, and a full description of what she is wearing."

Carlos talked for a long time, yet when he finished, both men were appalled at the small amount of real information they had listed. Gordon summed it up. "Wearing pale green voile dress. No real close friends in the city, merely acquaintances, and you have already inquired among them. Probably carrying less than two hundred dollars. Hmmm. Not a lot to go on—but enough to get started." He buzzed for his secretary. When the younger man entered, Gordon ordered, "Hood, cancel all my appointments for the rest of the day. We will be taking on Mr. O'Donnell's case." He knew he need add no more. Faithful Hood probably already knew more about the situation than his bland face showed.

"Very good, sir." Hood vanished and Gordon reached for his hat. "I'd like to see your sister's room," he told Carlos. "Is everything just as you found it?"

A dull red suffused Carlos face. "All but that

infernal bed sheet rope. My wife snatched it in so passers-by wouldn't see it." A glint of humor lit his dark eyes and again his newly hired attorney felt kinship with the proud man.

The comment also prepared him for Lorraine's icy welcome and her torrent of accusations against the missing bride-to-be. Good heavens, no wonder Miss O'Donnell fled! Listening to her sister-in-law's yammering would be enough to drive anyone mad.

The only clue they picked up in the deserted room was that a small amount of clothing had gone with the runaway.

"Oh, and the tapestry," Lorraine snapped.

"Tapestry?"

"A family heirloom," Carlos explained. The glance he gave his wife told Gordon this was a touchy issue. "It's very old and almost priceless."

"Then if Miss O'Donnell's finances get low, she will have something she can sell," Gordon observed.

"Tamar will never sell her tapestry," Carlos disagreed. "It's all she has left of our mother's."

"What is the tapestry like?"

"Red, green, and white, Mexico's national colors. Beautifully woven and about so big." He measured a rectangle in the air about three by four feet.

Gordon noted it. "Do you have a picture of her?"

Lorraine made a sound and Carlos fiercely turned toward her. She subsided, and he led Gordon downstairs and into the library. A lifelike replica of a young girl smiled into Gordon's eyes from among the other frowning portraits. "Why, she's lovely!"

He didn't realize he had spoken aloud until Lorraine's rasping voice taunted, "Oh yes, unless you have to live with her."

"Enough, woman." Carlos's patience was stretched thin by the continuing nightmare.

A secret grin came to Gordon's lips as he searched the picture for the "redheaded vixen" Lorraine described. Instead, he saw a sweet-faced girl with glowing dark eyes a shade lighter than her brother's, an innocent face framed by hair more gold than red. Mischief lurked in her eyes but not viciousness, spirit but not sulkiness. The artist had managed to capture far more than a physical likeness for a sort of spiritual aura surrounded the painted face. Gordon could almost see the curving lips set in determination, the white fingers doggedly knotting a rope from bed sheets. When she turned her back on the only home she had, had tears blinded the compelling eyes?

"And you planned to marry her to Carlin?" Gordon hadn't meant to say it, but the words spilled from his deep indignation.

Lorraine froze but Carlos stared at the portrait as if seeing it for the first time. When he silently faced Gordon, his eyes were dark with shame. "I see, now," he said.

"See what?" Lorraine shrilled. "Thanks to your precious sister, we're likely to be ruined. Phillip was here this morning and dug the truth out of me. He's threatening to sue for breach of contract."

"Sue whom?" Gordon's voice was rough. "The missing fiancee? You didn't sign any kind of papers, did you?"

"Of course not. Everything was verbal."

"Just what is this *everything*?"

Lorraine's eyes glittered like two shiny stones under green water. "When Tamar married him, Phillip was to receive a generous dowry. In addition, whatever she received under the conditions of her parents' will would naturally be his."

"You have no cause for concern," Gordon told the O'Donnells. "Any judge would throw the case out of court."

"I know that!" Lorraine glared as if she hated Gordon. "It's the ignominy of being taken to court with everyone laughing at us." Tears of fury drowned the gray-green eyes. She dabbed at them with a lace-edged handkerchief. "He said that if we would just go ahead and give him the dowry money he wouldn't sue."

"You didn't agree, I hope. If you did, he has a verbal contract." Gordon shuddered at the tangle that could ensue.

Angry color filled Lorraine's narrow face. "I am not a complete fool. I told him I could do nothing until I spoke with my husband."

"Thank God for that," Carlos put in.

"Mrs. O'Donnell, I don't think you need worry about either a court case or blackmail. I'll have to talk with Carlin. A few facts are in my possession concerning him that will make him eager to forget any harassment of you. Just one thing. To your knowledge, did Tamar—Miss O'Donnell—ever actually say she would marry Phillip?" He held his breath waiting for the reply.

"On the contrary, she said a hundred times she wouldn't." Lorraine sniffed. "He always seemed so pleasant, until today. Who could know he could change so rapidly?"

Carlos thoughtfully said, "Evidently Tamar knew or suspected. Rhys, I'll appreciate your doing what you can to silence him. Add your fee to whatever it requires to find Tamar."

Something in Gordon revolted. His gray eyes turned the color of ice. "We'll discuss the fee after we locate the runaway." He hesitated, then told Carlos, "I'd like you to accompany me on our visit to Carlin. A witness may come in handy."

"I wouldn't have it otherwise."

Less than a half hour later a man-servant ushered them into the luxurious suite Phillip had taken at a fine hotel. Carlin had seen no reason to leave, wedding or no wedding.

"Carlos. What a surprise." His eyes widened when he saw Gordon. By the time his visitors left, Phillip had abandoned his righteous indignation. He understood that he would be wise to no longer pursue hopes of money from the O'Donnells. The facts Gordon had used convinced the jilted groom that further intimidation of the O'Donnells would result in his expulsion from San Francisco society. "This is all Tamar's fault," was all he said, though his face was black with hatred.

"I had no idea what a rotter he is." A small white line encircled Carlos's set lips.

Gordon said nothing.

"I should have investigated before forcing Tamar into an engagement. I drove her away. I just hope someday I will be able to plead forgiveness." His voice actually shook. "Will it happen?"

Compassion replaced the lawyer's disgust. "Mr. O'Donnell, that is in God's hands."

"I-I haven't had a lot to do with God in the past years. I've been too busy making money." A spasm of pain crossed his face. He waited until they entered the closed carriage. "I've also blamed God for not sending me a son."

Gordon grasped what it cost Carlos to confess this. He kept his voice even. "We often give God credit for a lot of things and blame Him for even more. Until we realize the only way to live successfully is to accept His Son into our hearts, we can never have peace." He flushed. "Sorry for preaching."

"That's all right."

"Does your sister know God?"

"We both became Christians as children. I haven't talked to her about such things in years. I know she felt the shock of our parents' death, perhaps even more than I did. I buried myself in work, while she was uprooted when the family home was sold." Carlos looked at his hands. "I failed her."

"You know you can be forgiven."

"Yes. But can I forgive myself? Perhaps, when we find Tamar."

The desolation in his final words touched Gordon's warm heart. "How long do you think anyone as unusual as your sister can hide herself, especially with limited funds? Sooner or later, she will either have to come back or find work. When she does, it shouldn't be impossible to find her." Yet his words sounded hollow even to himself. What guarantee had they that Tamar would stay in San Francisco? Her inheritance might be small compared with Nob Hill standards, but it offered options Gordon preferred not to mention to Carlos. She could go a long way on $200—and who knew what direction she might choose?

No, Gordon decided. If I'm any judge of human nature, that girl won't run too far. He remembered something Carlos had said and inquired, "Will she try to contact your brother? You said they are close in years and devoted to one another."

Carlos shook his head. "Tamar will know that's the first person we'll consider."

"She might be smart enough to do a double double cross," Gordon reflected aloud. "By knowing you'll rule it out, that may be the very thing she'll do. Better get in touch with him."

"I will. I'll do anything," Carlos promised. His lips curved into a smile. "Even pray."

"Good." The carriage halted and Gordon sprang out. "We'll be in touch." He shook hands and sprinted into the office building and up the stairs. Hood met him at the door, his expression eager.

"Come in, Hood." Gordon stepped inside his own office and flung his hat in the general direction of a coat rack. "All right. This is what we have. Now tell me anything you know about Carlos O'Donnell, his wife, sister, and Phillip Carlin. It looks like we have one tough case in front of us."

All during the conference with Hood, Gordon scribbled notes, amazed as usual by the pale man's brilliance. He interrupted once with the irrelevant remark, "Why aren't you an attorney rather than a secretary?"

If Hood felt surprise at the question he masked it well. "I will be one day, sir. Just now I am learning as much as possible working for you." He smoothly went on with his recitation of Phillip Carlin's shortcomings, the O'Donnell holdings and pride, the reputed beauty of Tamar. "I've seen her a time or two with Carlin," Hood said and for a moment a human being peeped through the business machine. "She has a kind of—radiance. Any man would be proud to win her. It's hard to understand why her brother—or his wife—" He paused. "Why they would be willing to provide a dowry to Carlin, even though he does stand high with the society matrons on Nob Hill." A rare smile lit his face. "She has a certain charm that would be wasted on Carlin."

Gordon had been bending a letter opener back and forth. Now he threw it down in sudden decision. "Hood, how would you like to take charge of our search for this missing person? Right now I'm swamped with several cases coming up in court. I can't thrust them aside no matter how much I'd like to. I also know I can count on you to be totally discreet, no matter what you discover."

Hood sprang from his chair. All trace of pallor fled beneath the wave of excitement that showed in his eyes. "Sir, I'll do my best. But what about my other duties?"

"They can be reassigned." Gordon marveled at the change in the quiet young man. He leaned his chair back and clasped his hands behind his head. "Just for curiosity's sake, where will you begin?"

Again the mask of efficiency slipped and the eager boy showed through. "Miss O'Donnell sings, I believe? Perhaps she will secure a position as a music teacher."

Gordon laughed. "I can see your brain is already turning. Wish I had time to pursue this with you but if I don't finish preparing, an innocent man may be imprisoned." He bent to his work, barely conscious of Hood's leaving.

Less than a fortnight after Tamar's daring escape, Hood dragged into Gordon's office, face doleful. "Sir?"

Gordon glanced up from the piles of paper on his desk, his mind still on upcoming cases. Hood's first words, however, drove out all thought of even the most pressing duties.

"I've failed."

Gordon gasped. The look of misery on his secretary's face showed he didn't speak lightly. "You mean about finding Miss O'Donnell?"

Hood nodded and bit his lip, obviously perturbed. "Unless she's left San Francisco, she's better at hiding than I am at finding her." He spread his hands in a helpless gesture totally unlike his usual calm approach to the daily routine. "I followed up on your hunch she might pull a double double cross and contact her brother Richard, which I believe she did. I hotfooted it to his boarding school and could tell by the way he buttoned his lip that he knew something. He would have undergone an inquisition before telling me anything, though." A sheepish grin of admiration lightened his gloom. "Had to respect the kid. Anyway, I talked myself hoarse promising him we had Carlos's word Tamar wouldn't be hounded into marriage if she came back. The little devil raised one eyebrow and said, 'If I happen to hear from her, I'll pass on what you say.'" Hood's imitation brought a smile to Gordon's lips.

"Since then, nothing. If any of the elite had hired a music teacher, the servants would know. I've talked with them all, in addition to visiting the different schools that include musical instruction. No young lady with red-gold hair and dark eyes has even applied."

"What do we do now?" Gordon caught some of his secretary's heavy mood and his heart sank. He thought of the innocent girl alone and with dwindling funds, and his indignation against Phillip Carlin and Lorraine O'Donnell flared still hotter.

Perhaps that same indignation put new spirit into Hood. The younger man crossed his legs and a slow smile crossed his features. "We wait. Two hundred dollars can't keep her forever. Sooner or later, Miss Tamar O'Donnell is going to have to creep out from her hidey-hole and find work. When she does, we'll find her."

five

Tamar had left the solicitor's office feeling like a thief and despising herself for it. Mother and Father had left her the money, had they not? When the heavy fog lifted, so did her spirits, giving her the courage to march straight to the bank and cash her inheritance.

The friendly cashier almost proved to be her undoing. He counted out bills in cadence with a running monologue about her upcoming wedding, proud he recognized her from the rotogravures that had heralded the Carlin-O'Donnell nuptials.

"If 'twas me getting married and being a pretty young lady, I'd tuck this away as a nest egg," he babbled and failed to see her involuntary start. "Never know when a body will need to have a bit put aside of their own."

"Thank you," Tamar quietly said and slipped the money deep into her woven Mexican bag. As soon as she could get to a private place, she would hide the money in her garments. She forced herself to give the cashier a dazzling smile. "I might just take your advice."

She turned away, aware that his gaze followed her. Her heart thumped. The cashier would remember her, but she felt certain he would offer little information to those who came seeking her. She had seen the combination of wariness and sympathy in his eyes and wondered if his well-meaning comments were merely friendliness. Perhaps they were based instead on personal knowledge of Phillip-with-two-l's. She shrugged. What difference did it make? She had funds to keep her until she had time to find a plan.

First she must contact Dick. Her lips curved in a smile. Now that she'd escaped the oppressive Nob Hill mansion, life lay ahead as an adventure. Her part was to outguess her brother and Lorraine, Phillip, and anyone else who might trail her. They wouldn't believe she would dare to get in touch with Dick. Still, she must be careful.

A few hours later, tucked in a clean but plain second-story room in an obscure boarding house, Tamar struggled over a message that would tell Dick everything but others nothing. Her fingers ink-stained, she at last sat back and reread her epistle.

> *Dear Dick,*
>   *The bird you love flew out of the cage today. There's little chance of finding it, for it's sure to seek a nest of its own choosing. Don't worry about it—the wings were never clipped and now it can sing with joy.*

She left it unsigned. Dick knew her middle name

was Joy and would understand the symbolism of the rest of the note. She could imagine his wide grin when he read it and the way his black eyes would snap when he destroyed the seemingly harmless lines. Tamar sealed the note in an envelope, printed an address, and rode on a cable car to the end of the line before disembarking. She idled along an unfamiliar street to where she could post her note without attracting attention. She caught another car back, but made sure to get off several blocks from her new boarding place. A lump of loneliness in her throat, she crept back to her barren room and threw herself on the bed, determined to plan her course of action.

Tamar hadn't reckoned with the need her healthy young body had for sleep. The night before she had been too busy to close her eyes and now the release from strain tugged at her eyelids. "I'll sleep just a few minutes and. . . ."

She awoke to growing darkness and the kindly voice of her landlady calling, "Miss Darnell? Supper in fifteen minutes."

Darnell? Tamar struggled up through fathoms of sleep. Whose voice called and why did it say Darnell? Bewildered, still half asleep, a hasty glance around the unfamiliar room brought it all back. Tamar O'Donnell was now Joy Darnell, alone and friendless in a rented room.

No, not alone and not friendless. A verse learned at her mother's knee whispered in the weary girl's heart,

*I will be with thee, I will not fail thee nor forsake thee.** A rush of tears threatened. "God, are You here?" She hadn't really prayed since the train wreck. Now she slipped off the bed and to her knees. "Thank You for helping me this far. Please don't leave me. In Jesus's Name, amen."

She remained still for a moment, then got up and surveyed her meager wardrobe. A small smile brightened her face as she remembered how she had stowed her black clothing under a low-hanging tree, then claimed her inheritance wearing the green voile. She had worn it to the bank as well, then slipped behind thick branches and reappeared in her "crow" costume.

Now, her white waist and long dark skirt would do. She pulled her hair severely back and covered it with the hated veil. The black cloth dimmed her hair's gleam.

To her relief, Tamar found that the boarding house table held ample and well-cooked food. She was even more relieved that the widowed landlady made no effort to quiz her, and neither did the other boarders. If they wondered at her youth, they kept it to themselves and "Joy Darnell" slipped into their midst with less effect than a small pebble tossed in a pond.

Each morning Tamar left the boarding place, spent the day walking and thinking, then returned about the same time as the others, who all had jobs. She smiled a lot and said little. Even when the kind landlady patted her shoulder and remarked how nice it was to

*Joshua 1:5

have her there, Tamar only smiled.

A week passed. Two. Tamar faced a major decision. Should she pay for another fortnight? She'd been forced to make a few purchases and the money was growing low. She must work, but where? Finally, after much prayer, she boldly went to her landlady.

"I need a position," she said. "Could you write me a recommendation?"

"Of course, child. But why don't you get one from your present employers?" The good-hearted lady's brow wrinkled.

"I-I can't." She twisted her hands then looked up. "You see, the circumstances—"

"Don't say another word. I understand. Good girls like yourself don't have it easy in today's world. I'll wager you're running from some worthless man."

"In a way." She hated having to skirt the truth.

"What would you like to do? Care for children? Just this morning one of my ladies said she heard that Mrs. Wilson is frantic. She and her husband were all set for a trip and their children's companion quit without notice. The Wilsons need someone to look after four-year-old Dora and Donald—they're twins." She stopped talking long enough to rummage in a pile of papers until she found a clean sheet. "Let's see." She read aloud as she wrote, "Miss Darnell is a perfect lady and her character is beyond reproach. Anyone fortunate enough to have her in their home will rejoice over her gentility and quality." She signed it with a flourish, blew on it until the ink dried, then tucked it in an envelope. "This will do, I think, but I'm sorry to have you go."

"I must." Tamar bit her lip.

"You'll let me hear from you—and if things don't go right with the Wilsons, you come right back, you hear?"

"Thank you." She clutched the precious recommendation. No need to ask where the Wilsons lived. One of the newcomers to Nob Hill, they had purchased and refurbished a large mansion several blocks away from the O'Donnells. Did she dare work there? Why not? Though she knew of Mrs. Wilson, she had never met her—and the last place Carlos or Lorraine would seek for her would be in the nursery of a home in their own neighborhood.

She thought of the wealth of trousseau clothes she had left behind and sighed. Being limited to what she had been able to bring with her had its drawbacks. She had been forced to buy a second waist to go with her dark skirt—but wouldn't children prefer to see something lighter? Tamar sighed. Perhaps by summer she could get a position farther away and dare to wear her green voile—but not now. "Some bright ribbon will help," she decided. "I can make rosettes and wear them for color." With a prayer for help, she tremulously made her way to the Wilsons.

"What a godsend," fluffy little Mrs. Wilson gasped. She barely read the recommendation, fired a dozen questions concerning Tamar's experience with children, and fortunately didn't wait for answers, then wound up in the nursery where two placid cherubs with flaxen hair and blue eyes played quietly with their toys. When their mother announced that Miss Darnell would be their new companion, their lack of surprise told Tamar she was neither the first nor would she be the last newcomer.

"And I'm sure you'll have a perfectly lovely time together," Mrs. Wilson concluded. "Miss Darnell, your meals will be served up here with the children's." She laughed nervously. "After all, a children's companion is a step above the servants, although of course you won't be served with the rest of the family."

Tamar wanted to laugh. How stunned her new employer would be if she knew she had delegated Carlos O'Donnell's sister to eat in the nursery! Amused at the snobbish but inflexible rule, she murmured, "Of course." The less she had to do with the other adults in the house, the less chance there would be that someone might recognize her. Dora and Donald would give her some companionship, and the library she passed with Mrs. Wilson would keep her well occupied during any leisure hours.

Mrs. Wilson noticed her glance through the library's open doors. "Feel free to read anything you like," she invited. "When we return you'll need to be careful not to disturb my husband when he is in the library. But for the next few months, you may go in any time."

Again Tamar felt like laughing at the pretentious little woman who could be so insulting and never know it.

"Now, how soon can you come? Today?"

Tamar hesitated. They hadn't discussed money. She swallowed her O'Donnell pride and asked, "What is the remuneration?"

Mrs. Wilson glanced at the patrician chin above the plain black cloak, the steady eyes, then named a figure a good deal higher than Tamar had expected. She paused to silently thank the Heavenly Father she was learning to rely on.

The society woman evidently mistook her hesitation for a bid for a higher wage. "You understand this is just for the time we'll be gone. Once we get back, if everything has gone satisfactorily—which of course it will—we will raise the figure by ten dollars a month."

Red flags flew in Tamar's cheeks, but she simply nodded and said, "I will go for my things and return this afternoon."

"Can't we send for them?"

Tamar felt a little thrill. Mrs. Wilson didn't want her to get away. After Lorraine's coldness, Tamar was warmed by the knowledge that someone wanted her. "I promise I'll come."

Relief made the little woman more fluttery than

ever. "Good. We'll expect you. You'll have the room next to the children's and share their bathroom. You won't have to do any cleaning, just be with the children. We'll arrange for the second maid to relieve you one afternoon a week and on Sunday morning, if you care to attend church." She actually accompanied her new children's companion to the door. "Miss Darnell, I truly believe Divine Providence has led you to us in our hour of need." She clapped her hands.

"I do, too, Mrs. Wilson." Tamar thought about it all the way to her boarding house. She had no experience with God arranging people's lives and yet, at least so far, things had turned out well for her.

The Wilsons departed the next day, and Tamar began her new position. "What do you like to do?" she asked Dora and Donald.

"Whatever you do," they told her.

"Then what are some of the things your other companions had you do?" she asked, determined to get beneath their calm surface. Even her meager experience with four-year-olds told her these two were unusually well-behaved—or were they cowed?

Eventually, Dora and Donald, reassured by her genuine concern, confided that their previous companions had simply parked the children in the nursery, told them to play with their toys, then settled down with books that Tamar suspected were trashy novels.

"We're going to be different," she announced. Four

blue eyes sparkled when she counted off on her fingers the games they would play, the walks they would take, and the simple lessons they would learn. Tamar drew on the store of her own rich childhood for ideas. Busy as they were, Mother and Father still had taken time to play with her and teach her about the wonderful world. As a result, she was able to make Dora and Donald's faces grow rosy with color. Their childish laughter livened up the mansion until even the servants joined in the plans to make their dwelling place happy.

"She's a dandy, she is." The cook put their feelings into words. "Never looks down her pretty nose. Never asks a thing for herself, just a picnic lunch for the children sometimes." She sniffed. "Too good to last. We'll never keep that one. Not like the others, a pox on them, mealy-mouthed and holding too good an opinion of themselves as what aren't no better than the rest of us."

Tamar had been coming toward the kitchen but stopped at the first words. She stuffed her hand in her mouth and tiptoed back to her own room before the giggles exploded. Nob Hill society might be scandalized by Tamar O'Donnell's leaving Phillip at the altar, but Nob Hill servants had taken Miss Darnell to their hearts.

October became November and then in turn December. In spite of an ever-present ache in her heart, Tamar managed to be content with the children. She tactfully handled a potentially sticky situation when Dora sighed and said, "With Mummy and Daddy gone, we won't have a Christmas."

"Won't have Christmas," Donald added, blue eyes sad.

The children's passive acceptance of their parents' neglect went straight to Tamar's heart. Visions of her own happy holidays set her smiling lips into a determined line. "We'll see about it," she told the children in her most mysterious voice. "Now run along for your naps." She thrilled when four chubby arms grabbed her and soft lips pressed her cheeks. In the weeks since she came to the Wilsons, she had learned to love Dora and Donald. Now she considered for a moment, then timidly walked downstairs and entered the kitchen.

The cook looked up with a smile. "Is it a picnic lunch you'll be wanting, miss?" A bevy of servants also smiled at her.

Tamar shook her head. "No, I need to ask you about Christmas. Did the Wilsons make any arrangements?"

"Just to see that there's a good dinner ready before we go to our own families," the cook said. "If it's all right with you, we thought we could serve Christmas dinner early, perhaps even at three or four o'clock?" The faces turned toward Tamar showed longing for a little extra time for merrymaking.

"Why can't we have our main meal right at noon?" Tamar impulsively suggested. "That way you can clear away and have the rest of the day free." She cocked her head and added, "I'm sure there will be plenty of food left and the twins and I will raid the pantry for supper."

Loud cries of approval encouraged Tamar to go on. "If it isn't too much trouble, do you think we could have a little party on Christmas Eve?" She caught the apprehensive looks of the staff.

"Who would you be wanting to invite, miss?"

Tamar's eyes widened. "Oh, no one! I meant a party just for us and the children, with a tree and gifts—the Wilsons did leave presents, didn't they?"

The housekeeper nodded. "The mistress and master's wardrobe are filled with packages."

"Perhaps we should wait and give them to the twins on Christmas Day. I'll find a few things for Christmas Eve," Tamar planned.

"So will we." Distrust gone, the servants gathered around Tamar, and in the next few weeks, they often whisked things out of sight when she appeared. A few days before the holiday, Tamar sought out the cook. "I-I didn't think of it before, but the Wilsons might not like it if we used the drawing room for our party."

"Don't fret yourself. We'll put up the tree, pretty as you please, in the drawing room for Christmas Day— but the chauffeur and maids are already decorating the servants' dining room for our Christmas Eve party." She sniffed. "The Wilsons might not approve of the children being there, but they can't object when they aren't here where they belong. Fine thing, going off at Christmas and leaving the little ones." A broad smile made creases in her round face. "If master or mistress raises a rumpus about Dora and Donald eating with the servants for once, we'll just up and tell 'em we knew they wouldn't want the likes of us stepping out of our places." She cast a shrewd glance at Tamar. "I'm for thinking you'll be wanting your Christmas dinner in the nursery, as usual?"

"I think that's best." Glad for the understanding woman, Tamar cast off her worries. "We'll just go into the drawing room long enough for the children to receive the presents their parents left." Mischief danced in her dark eyes. "*I'm* for thinking we'll have a lot happier time on Christmas Eve with all of you."

The Christmas conspiracy securely glued the staff's friendship with the new companion. Such whispering and planning—and not just on the servants' part. Tamar helped the twins make gifts for every member of the staff—nothing that cost money, but carefully colored pictures from chubby fingers, pasted on cardboard with scraps of bright materials. She pretended blindness when Dora hastily covered a special picture she had been working on, and she acted as if she had no clue to why Donald asked what her favorite colors were. Out of her carefully guarded inheritance money she bought inexpensive pictures of the manger scene for the twins and servants. Cook had promised to bake a Christmas "birthday" cake in honor of the Christ child, and as part of the celebration, Tamar meant to tell the story of Jesus's coming to earth.

At last December twenty-fourth came, a heavenly blue and gold day with a crisp wind coming in off the bay. Tamar and the children had a good frolic in the garden after lunch and then the twins obediently trotted off for naps. "You'll want to be all rested for tonight," she told them. "Something nice is going to happen."

"What, Miss Joy?" At Tamar's invitation, the twins had long since dropped "Darnell" from her name.

"It's a Christmas surprise." She gently pushed Donald back onto the pillow and pulled a blanket over Dora. Downstairs, the drawing room with its formal tree and expensive toys stood closed. The servants' dining room with a smaller, friendlier tree glowed with firelight, gaslight, and cheer. Popcorn and cranberries and bright paper ornaments hung from its spicy-smelling branches and tissue-wrapped packages awaited the eager clutch of small fingers.

"Why, I'm almost happy," Tamar murmured. "I wonder—is it because I've been busy working to make others happy?" The idea hovered like a winged moth while she smuggled her own carefully prepared gifts out of her room and downstairs. The camaraderie of the shirt-sleeved butler and aproned cook, the

busy housekeeper and giggling maids welcomed her
and warmed her heart, making her feel she had found
a real home and an adopted family.

six

Soft tears dripped into Tamar's lap and she hastily wiped them away, but not before Donald noticed.

"Miss Joy, are you sad?" He crept close to her, all the wonder and excitement of the "Christmas surprise" eclipsed by worry.

"No, I'm happy." She hugged him and smiled.

Dora chimed in, "I'm happy, too. This is the bestest Chris'mas in the whole world." She patted the little mound of gifts in her lap. "Cook made mittens for us just like yours." She pointed to those on the floor beside Tamar and wiggled her red wool fingers.

Tamar looked up from the low stool where she sat surrounded by evidence of the staff's friendship. "I can never thank you enough." She felt tears coming again and hesitated.

"It's you we should be thanking," the cook said and held up the pictures the twins had made, then the one of the manger scene. "'Tis the happiest Christmas this house has known and I've been here for many a day." Heads nodded in agreement. "A shame, it is, to have it be over."

Tamar slowly rose and faltered, "I was going to tell the children the story of the first Christmas tomorrow, but—"

"Tell it now," Dora pleaded and clutched her skirts.

The housekeeper fingered her picture of the Nativity. "I wouldn't mind hearing it—not all of us will be going to church." A wistful note in her voice was echoed by the look in some of the others' faces.

"Let's sing some of the carols I've been teaching the twins," Tamar said. Soon the room rang with the familiar melodies of "Joy to the World," "Hark the Herald Angels Sing," and "Oh Come All Ye Faithful." The butler thoughtfully turned down the gaslight and Tamar sent him a look of gratitude. Perhaps the dimmer light would hide her trembling hands. She had never before told anyone the story of the birth of Christ, but a quick prayer steadied her. She began by reading the beautiful story from the second chapter of Luke, remembering her mother's voice from years gone by. The twins sat entranced, chins in hands, blue eyes wide. Someone cleared his throat, but for the most part, her listeners sat quietly.

Now what? she frantically thought when she ended with the age-old cry of praise, *Glory to God in the highest, and on earth peace, goodwill toward men.* Then into the little pool of silence came voices singing softly, "Silent night, holy night." For a moment Tamar wondered if she were hearing things.

"All is calm, all is bright." The song grew louder.

"It's the carolers, miss." The butler went to the window and threw it wide. Perfect harmony deepened the meaning of the familiar words; Tamar felt she might burst with the realization of what that first Christmas meant to a sinful world. A twin on each side of her, she strained her ears to catch the final, lovely chord. Then cries of, "Happy Christmas!" floated in the open window.

"Happy Christmas to you," those inside the mansion called. Lanterns waved and the little band of carolers moved on, leaving their words of hope and cheer glowing in Tamar's heart like a luminous star.

As usual, the cook took the lead. She surveyed the others, motioned to the children, and said, "Don't you ever be forgetting Whose birthday this is." Enjoyment shone in every syllable. "Just to make sure, I've baked a cake, at Miss Joy's suggestion." The cake was four layers high, with a single candle in the middle of its gleaming white frosting. The twins oohed and ahed. Not until they had finished every delicious crumb, did Tamar reluctantly say, "This has been wonderful but it's bedtime." She ruefully looked at the disheveled table. "As soon as I put the children to bed I'll come down and help straighten up."

"Indeed you won't," the housekeeper retorted. "There are plenty of us to care for things below stairs. You've done enough." Tamar gave in with another smile of appreciation and herded her excited charges upstairs. They took a long time to fall asleep and when they did, she slipped down to the servants' dining room. Except for the tree, everything stood in its usual shining order, and the table had been laid for breakfast. A quick trip to the kitchen showed the same. With a light step, Tamar climbed the long staircase to her own room, again aware of the strange tug she had felt earlier.

"God," she prayed when she had disrobed and donned her long nightgown. "Thank You for bringing me here. But thank You most of all for the gift of your precious Son. I pray that You will help me teach Dora and Donald about Him. In Jesus's Name, amen." She turned on her side, looked out the long window at the moonlit world, and added, "Please, God, help me keep the peace I feel tonight and someday help Carlos—and Lorraine—to know You."

Christmas Day sped by. Tamar eyed the expensive toys left by the Wilsons and remembered how she also had been given such things. Yet few gifts had touched her as deeply as the simple offerings from her fellow-workers. In honor of the holiday, she wore ribbon rosettes at her collar and let her red-gold hair hang free for the first time since she fled the O'Donnell mansion. The staff gasped at the change it made in her but wisely said nothing. If Miss Joy wished to disguise her beauty by keeping her curls in place and hidden, so be it. The butler stolidly served dinner and by one o'clock, all the servants were ready to depart.

"I'm not happy about leaving you alone," the housekeeper told Tamar. "If my mother weren't old and expecting me, I wouldn't go off and have you here just with the children."

Tamar patted her arm. "I'll lock the doors if it makes you feel better," she promised. "Besides, what could happen? If I need anything, there are plenty to help me." She waved out the door at the nearby mansion across the way. A full score of carriages stood in its curving drive.

"Well, all right." The older woman stepped outside. "I'll be home by eight at the latest."

"Happy Christmas." Tamar closed and locked the door, then gathered the children. "Shall we take some of your new toys to the nursery? It's easier to play there."

"Yes, Miss Joy." Donald and Dora willingly helped her. A little later, though, they tired of their new possessions and came to the low rocker where Tamar sat reading. The Wilson library had opened her eyes to the world of knowledge, and she devoured a variety of books in her free time.

"Will you please tell us a story?" they pleaded.

She moved to a larger rocker, one big enough to hold all three of them. "What would you like to hear?'

"Tell us s'more about Baby Jesus," Dora ordered and Tamar's heart leaped. In low, even tones she repeated every story she could remember until the children's eyelids drooped. "Time for your afternoon nap," she told them gently.

"If I'm going to tell them stories about Jesus, I need

a Bible of my own," she decided. "The one I've been reading from the Wilsons' library is so large and heavy, it's hard to hold." Pleasant thoughts crept into her mind, and the huge Christmas dinner left her drowsy. She slipped to her room, removed her shoes, and lay down on the bed. Her last waking thought concerned her next free afternoon. Perhaps the children would enjoy going with her while she bought her Bible.

The wintry darkness of late afternoon shadowed the walls when she awakened. *Something is wrong.* She lay rigid, alert, waiting for whatever had woken her to sound again. A quick spring from bed to the open door of the twins' room showed nothing out of the ordinary. A clock chimed and she counted its strokes. Five, far too few to herald the return of any of the staff. Yet—she froze. A sound, the same sliding sound she realized must have disturbed her, came again, then the sound of heavy footsteps below.

Fear gripped her throat. She automatically glanced out the window and noted in despair that the carriages lining the neighbors' drive a few hours earlier had vanished. The closest mansion sat dark and inscrutable. No help there.

"Standing here isn't going to solve anything," she whispered. "Get going, Tamar O'Donnell." Flinging her sleep-tangled curls back, she looked about for a weapon, settled on a heavy poker, and noiselessly left her room, prepared to defend the children against the intruder.

The great hall below the staircase lay in shadow. Tamar paused at the top and peered into the darkness. A tall and blacker shadow detached itself from the library entrance and stumbled into a piece of furniture. Tamar stifled a gasp, whispered a prayer, and glided down the stairs like a wisp of fog. The figure stood facing away from her. She lowered her voice to a hoarse whisper, hoping the intruder would take her for the butler, then jabbed the poker between the prowler's shoulder blades.

"Raise your hands and don't move," she hissed.

"What the. . . ." Two hands shot into the air.

"Walk straight toward the door." She prodded harder with her weapon, wondering what she would do if the unwelcome visitor refused. "And don't speak." From the intruder's voice, she knew she had a man to deal with, one much larger than she. The element of uncertainty as to who she was and what dug into his back offered her and the children their only protection, frail as it might be.

He preceded her in the direction she guided until she knew he had reached the door.

"Unlock it and go." She kept her voice in the same tone. Sensing his resistance, she again pressed on her weapon.

He grunted, fumbled with the heavy key and lock, then swung the door wide and stepped outside.

Tamar slammed the door behind him. Her knees

felt more quivery than the cranberry jell she had eaten for Christmas dinner.

A loud knock stiffened them. Mercy, was he trying to get back in? She felt the doorknob turn beneath her shaking fingers and for a moment couldn't remember if she'd had the presence of mind to lock the door after she slammed it. She had and it held. But an angry voice demanded,

"Let me in, you fool. Don't you know who I am?"

All Tamar knew was that she had never heard the voice before. "Go away or it will be the worse for you," she ordered.

Even the heavy door couldn't drown his curses. "I'll have you dismissed if you don't open the door this minute." Another thundering knock came.

"God, what can I do?" she frantically prayed. This time she didn't answer, just leaned against the door in fear, as if her pressing hands could lend the door strength.

The pounding went on, interspersed with threats. Minutes or an eternity later, the sound of carriage wheels brought Tamar a wave of relief. Thank God, someone had come.

"Why, Mr. Edgar, what are you doing here?" The housekeeper's surprised question sounded muffled.

"Why is this door locked? And where are my sister's servants, off gallivanting while she's gone? The lights aren't even on. Where are Donald and Dora?"

"Sound asleep in their beds, I'd hope, sir. Miss Joy probably didn't hear you knock. She and the children had noon dinner so the rest of us could have a bit of extra time off. I got to worrying over them and came back early."

"She?"

Tamar heard the disbelief in his voice and hastily unlocked the door and flung it wide. Before the two on the doorstep could come inside, she quickly turned up the gaslight, then blinked in its bright rays.

"Oh, there you are, Miss Joy. Mr. Edgar here wasn't expected and—"

"Stop blathering, woman." Edgar glared at Tamar, who stood speechless before him, red-gold hair hanging in confusion about her patrician face, dark eyes flashing. His expression changed, and he swept her a glance from the crown of her beautiful head down her slender figure.

She felt her face scorch and drew herself up. "In the future, I suggest that you enter your sister's home by the front door," she icily told him.

The housekeeper looked bewildered. "Is there trouble here?"

Tamar hid the poker behind her and said nothing.

Edgar had the grace to mumble, "When no one came and I found the door locked, I raised a window and—I don't have to answer to you, either of you." He haughtily lifted his chin.

"Miss Joy, where are you?" A call came from the

nursery.

"The noise has awakened the twins." Tamar squared her shoulders and turned. "If you'll excuse me, I'll see to them." She mounted the stairs like a queen at her coronation.

"*That's* the children's companion?"

Tamar shivered with foreboding. Something in Edgar's manner made her feel unclean. The housekeeper's crisp retort did nothing to reassure her. "She's not like the others, Mr. Edgar. Leave this one alone."

"You forget your place." Frost hung on every word, and Tamar turned her head just enough to see the housekeeper scuttle away. Her heart sank. Last night and today she had felt the Wilson mansion close to Eden in its perfection. Edgar's appearance cast a shadow across her new-found paradise.

"I'll just have to stay out of his way," she determined and went to reassure the twins. After they were tidied for supper, the housekeeper came and tapped on her door furtively. "I was just thinking perhaps— with Mr. Edgar here and all—would you like me to bring a tray rather than foraging as you had planned?"

"I would appreciate it very much," Tamar told her.

"It's just for tonight. He never stays long and the other servants will be back soon and oh dear, why did he have to come now? What actually happened?"

Tamar quietly told her what had occurred.

The housekeeper's lips set in a grim line. "Miss

Joy, I hope you don't think I'm meddling but if I were you, I would put my hair back up in its usual way." She flushed and started to withdraw, but Tamar laid a hand on her arm.

"Thank you. I understand perfectly."

The tray contained enough party food and mugs of hot chocolate topped with whipped cream to satisfy the twins. Upset as she felt, Tamar forced herself to eat for their sake. Then she curiously said, "Tell me about your Uncle Edgar."

Dora shook her flaxen head. "He's bad."

"Bad," Donald echoed, a white cream ring around his mouth. "Daddy said if Uncle Edgar didn't be good he couldn't come here. Mummy cried."

Their companion's need to know the worst overcame her distaste at pumping the children. "Why is he bad?"

"We don't know," Dora admitted. "But before you came, I saw him kissing the other lady. Then she went away. A long time ago," she added vaguely.

Tamar felt her blood chill. In spite of her sheltered upbringing, she knew a bit of the world. If only Edgar hadn't seen her with her hair down! Would today's incident result in her having to leave? A pang filled her. Just when she had begun to find happiness. She hoped his anger at being ousted by a young woman with a poker would cool any ardor toward her he might possess. She had grown to love Dora and Donald and they had responded freely. Must a selfish young aristocrat spoil everything by forcing unwanted attentions on her?

Her worst fears were realized a little later when Edgar barged into the nursery unannounced. "Well, hello, dear niece and nephew." He produced packages from behind his back and bestowed them on the children. They showed little enthusiasm for the costly toys that duplicated what they already had.

A resigned look came to Dora's face and she said, "Miss Joy was going to tell us a story."

"Story," Donald repeated, and climbed into Tamar's lap.

Hair back in the severe style she had adopted when she went into service, Tamar welcomed Donald and made room for Dora. She didn't quite dare tell a Bible story; instead, she held the children spellbound with a tale of an imaginary elf who lived beneath a rock and got into all kinds of predicaments. She didn't give the fourth member of the little party so much as a look until both children drowsed.

"Perhaps you had better go," she quietly told the man. In an odd way he reminded her of Phillip-with-two-l's, although Edgar's short stature and resemblance to his sister was nothing like the other man.

"I'll take Donald." He bent low and she jerked her head back to avoid contact with his mocking face.

"I c'n walk." Donald solved her problem by sliding off her lap and weaving toward his bed, forcing Edgar away from Tamar.

"Please go." She gracefully rose with Dora.

Storm clouds gathered in his petulant face. "May I remind you this is my sister's home?"

The same natural dignity that had quelled the junior law partner once more came to her aid. "I am in charge of this nursery, sir. I am asking you to leave. Now."

A sneer curled his lips. "I can have you replaced."

"Until you do, I am still in charge here. Out!" To her utter amazement he marched to the doorway. An ugly look and an unintelligible mutter remained in her memory long after he vanished.

The week between Christmas and New Year's became a nightmare. If she had not given her word to care for the twins, she would have left the Wilsons' house. The strain of dodging Edgar made her lose weight and her eyes grew haunted. The staff rallied and helped her as much as they could, but they could do little when Edgar insisted on visiting the nursery. He dogged her steps when she took the children out, paying her fulsome compliments. When he demanded her presence at dinner, she coldly told him she ate with the children. He insisted that he was the master of his house in his sister and brother-in-law's absence, and commanded her to dine with him. Tamar ignored his edicts.

But she couldn't ignore his actions on New Year's Eve. Emboldened by too much liqueur, he lurched up the stairs, beat on Tamar's locked door, and shouted for her to let him in.

The children must not suffer from their uncle's anger at her, Tamar realized. She stuffed her hair under her veil, wrapped herself in a dark dressing gown, and opened the door so suddenly it caught him off guard. He tumbled into a heap.

"What is the meaning of this?" She kept her voice low.

"Want a little kiss goo'night." He grinned up at her foolishly. She shrank away as he got to his feet and reached for her.

She must get him away from the children's room. Step by step she backed down the hall. Once she reached the staircase, a quick slide down the banister rail would take her to freedom. By the time he could get downstairs, she'd have reached the safety of the servants' quarters.

"Joy, pretty, pretty Joy," he singsonged, hands outstretched like a sleepwalker.

God, help me. She quickened her steps, reached the spot where the hall and staircase intersected, and hopped onto the banister rail. With a cry of triumph, Edgar staggered toward her—and missed. His waving arms met the empty air behind her.

Down, down, she slid. Her pursuer weaved after her down the stairs. She thudded to a halt and flew across the hall. An awful cry behind her brought her to a stop. Thump, thump, thump. Edgar had successfully navigated two-thirds of the stairs but his momentum proved too much for his condition. Balance gone, he slipped, fell, and landed in a crumpled heap at the bottom.

seven

Horror-stricken, Tamar couldn't move. The sound of racing feet brought her to her senses. "Miss Joy, what is it?" the butler cried. The anxious cook, housekeeper, and other staff members joined them, some still struggling into dressing gowns.

"He-he pounded at my door. I didn't want him to wake the twins." Tamar found only sympathy and concern for her in the watching eyes. Even in the middle of tragedy, a rush of gladness roughened her voice; not since her parents had died had she felt so loved. "I ran from him, slid down the banister rail and he followed down the stairs. . . ." Her voice trailed off when the butler brushed past her and knelt beside the fallen figure.

"He isn't badly hurt, just has a bump on his head. See, he's already coming around, the drunken lout."

A little murmur of assent rippled through the staff.

"Begging your pardon, Miss Joy, but you won't want to be here when he rouses." The cook firmly led Tamar past the huddled man. "Like as not, Mr. Edgar won't even remember what happened. Lock yourself in with the children and forget all this. We'll see he's cared for, though he doesn't deserve it."

Tamar obediently climbed the long staircase but forgetting proved impossible. "I can't stay, you know."

"I s'pose not. You won't be the first to leave because of that—that—" Words failed the irate cook. "You *will* be the first to resent his attentions." She waited until Tamar reached her room. Brow furrowed, she reluctantly said, "If you feel you must go it will be well to get away come morning." She sniffed in her most eloquent way. "He won't be up and around until at least noon."

"What about Dora and Donald?" Tamar asked. "The Wilsons won't be home for another few days."

The cook shrugged. "The housekeeper's looked after them before and will again." She sighed loudly. "Where will you go?"

"I don't know yet," Tamar said dully.

"Do you have any money? I don't mean to pry, but you must have spent a good deal for the Christmas gifts, and—"

"I'll have enough." She threw her arms around the good woman. "You've all been so kind." She choked back tears. "You'll never know how much I hate to go but being in the house with that man is impossible."

Settled back into her bed but far from sleep, Tamar reiterated what she'd told the cook. She couldn't stay under any circumstances. The look in Edgar's face had made clear that he considered his sister's employees as opportunities for sport. She shivered, cold to her very soul. Would she have to face the same attitude elsewhere? If so, perhaps she had better go somewhere and simply starve when her money ran out.

Long before daylight, Tamar stood packed and ready. She had written the notes she would leave behind her. One for the twins—"Darlings, I have to go away. Always remember what a happy Christmas we had and the stories of the Baby Jesus. As you grow, learn to known Him, for He will be your best Friend."

The second, to Mrs. Wilson. Her ingrained honesty scorned making excuses. "I regret leaving without notice but the unwelcome attentions of your brother forces me to do so." She signed it, "Joy Darnell," and a tear blotted the page. How would the Wilsons react to the news? Edgar would surely lie to smooth it over. Yet Mr. Wilson must suspect the truth about his brother-in-law, or he would not have threatened to keep Edgar from coming to the house. Perhaps Mr. Wilson would speak with the staff and learn the truth.

"God, thank You that the reference from my landlady has no date," she prayed. "I can use it and say nothing about ever working here."

A soft tap at the door sent Tamar across the room on quiet feet. She did not want to wake Dora and Donald in the next room. "Who is it?"

"Cook says you're to come right down. The

chauffeur is to take you where you wish to go but you're to have breakfast first," the housekeeper whispered when Tamar cracked opened the door.

She started to protest, then reconsidered. She gathered up her little store of belongings, a few more than when she had arrived at the Wilsons. A last glance at the twins brought a lump to her throat but she swallowed hard and turned away. Perhaps someday God would allow her to see them again. Until then, "Please, keep them in Your care," she prayed.

To her surprise, every member of the staff had crowded into the big kitchen, although the hour was far earlier than the one when they usually began their day. They hovered over Tamar, urging her to eat another hot biscuit, pointing to the enormous basket of food the cook had somehow found time to prepare. She forced herself to eat for their sake.

When she finished, the kindly cook spoke. "Here's a bit of a present and 'tis sorry we are you're leaving." She thrust a sealed envelope into Tamar's hands and blinked. "A pox on Mr. Edgar for being what he is!"

Tamar managed a smile. She felt she should protest the gift, for she knew it was money they could ill afford to give. Yet a little voice warned her to be a gracious receiver. She faltered, though, when she looked around the circle of friendly faces. "You know I wouldn't go if I didn't have to." She bit her lip. "I've learned to love you all."

"You'll let us know when you're relocated?" the

housekeeper asked.

Tamar nodded and followed the chauffeur out into gray pre-dawn gloom that softened trees and bushes into ghostly, distorted things. "Where shall I take you, miss?" he inquired.

The only safe haven she could think of was her old boarding house. She gave the address and listlessly leaned her tired head against the window. If no vacant room were available, she'd have to think of something else.

The carriage stopped, and the chauffeur helped her to the street. "Not one of us will tell Ed-the Wilsons where you are," he promised.

"Thank you." Tamar held out her hand and he awkwardly shook it, then followed her to the door. Light from the kitchen window cast a golden glow into the gloom. "I'll be all right. You know God will look after me."

"That He will, miss." The chauffeur bowed and turned away. "I'd best be getting back before the fireworks pop."

She watched the carriage out of sight before rapping at the door.

A few days at the boarding house were followed by a few weeks as a children's companion in another home. This time the master of the house caught Tamar in the back hall and pinioned her arms. She twisted her head away from his kisses, let fly with a sturdy shoe, and he was forced to explain the sudden limp he acquired. He also had to explain to his suspicious wife the sudden departure of "the best children's companion we ever had."

"Dearie," her landlady told her. "Why don't you give up trying to be a companion and use that sweet voice I hear singing sometimes? You'd earn more and goodness knows, you could simply give lessons in your room, if you like."

Tamar thought about it. Again her funds had dwindled. The generous gift from the Wilsons' staff brought a mist of gratitude to her heart whenever she thought of it, but that too was nearly gone. She finally decided to try the landlady's suggestion.

After more consideration, however, she made up her mind that her present lodging place lay too close to those she sought to elude. One afternoon she bid her tearful landlady farewell and left San Francisco for the growing city of Oakland, three miles across San Francisco Bay to the east. Heart pounding, she inspected a dozen places before selecting a room in a respectable place recommended by her San Francisco landlady. Her faith in God opened doors, and despite her lack of formal training, her singing talent secured her a position with a music school. Her job consisted of learning songs the pupils would be taught and demonstrating how they should be sung.

When late in January the school director summoned her to her office, Tamar obeyed with her heart thumping. Had her services proved unacceptable?

She enjoyed singing and the past few days had begun to relax and feel comfortable. With a quick prayer, she tapped on the partly-opened door of the director's office.

"Come in."

Tamar stepped inside, glanced at the ample-figured director, then at the woman who sat in a chair next to the desk. Rich furs spoke of her wealth. So did a patrician chin and long, slim hands.

"Miss Darnell, Mrs. Gregory overheard you singing when she brought Mistress Alice in for her lesson. She asked to speak to you."

Tamar resisted the urge to remind her employer that persons speak *to* dogs and cats but *with* other adults. The Mrs. Gregories of the world probably considered servants and singing teachers lower on the social scale than household pets.

"I'll leave you to have your little chat." The instructor hoisted herself from her chair and motioned Tamar to sit, then heavily strode to the door and closed it behind her.

"You really have a sweet little voice, Miss Darnell." The patronizing tone brought Tamar's gaze back to the visitor.

"Thank you." She kept her voice colorless and refused to be cowed by the other's rude stare.

"I'm having a party for Alice's eighth birthday," Mrs. Gregory said. "Naturally, we'll have the best families from Oakland and San Francisco." She paused to let her importance sink in.

Tamar wanted to ask whose party it was, Mrs. Gregory's or Alice's, but again she forced herself to keep silent.

"Tell me, does young Alice show promise? We've had her to so many different schools it's hard to know what to believe."

Tamar felt her interest rise. While Alice's mother did not impress her, she genuinely cared for Alice. "Mrs. Gregory, while Alice doesn't appear to show signs of becoming a great opera singer, she has a clear, beautiful voice that can enrich her life and bring pleasure to many."

The woman's haughty guard lowered. "Thank you for your honesty, Miss Darnell." She leaned forward. "Would you be willing to come to our home and stay with us for a few weeks, so Alice can have your exclusive attention? I'd so love for her to perform at the party."

Tamar could scarcely believe her own ears. "Why—"

"I took the liberty of asking what you are paid," Mrs. Gregory confessed. "I'll be happy to triple the amount. Your job here will be waiting when you finish with Alice." She raised a delicate eyebrow when Tamar didn't jump at the chance. "I do hope you won't need time to consider it. The party is really coming up quite soon."

Tamar mentally tabulated her little store of money and weighed it against the danger of being recognized at the Gregories'. The danger should be small. Family or acquaintances would hardly expect to find her in Oakland. "I'll come."

"Thank you, Miss Darnell. I'm sure Alice will be overjoyed. She's grown quite fond of you even in the short time you've been here." Mrs. Gregory rose with a swish of taffeta, beaming. She started for the door, then turned back to Tamar. "Oh, if all goes well with Alice, her father and I will be happy to give you a good recommendation should you ever tire of working for the school. I'm sure several of our friends would be glad to find someone like you and be spared the tiresome task of going from school to school." She flowed out without waiting for a reply.

Tamar dropped back into the chair and laughed. In spite of Mrs. Gregory's patronage, she rather liked the woman. "I'll do my best with Alice," she vowed.

"Good for you." The instructor came in with an alacrity that hinted she'd been hovering just outside the door. "Keep the songs she is to sing simple, as befits her young age. Ballads, folk songs, even a hymn would be appropriate." Her tired face took on a conspiratorial expression. "People like the Gregories pretend to like the classics but secretly prefer something they can understand."

A little more than two weeks later, Tamar bitterly regretted ever having heard of the Gregories, even appealing Alice. Alice should have been dressing to sing at the party, but instead she lay feverish and miserable with a cold. Mrs. Gregory had refused to believe the hoarseness wouldn't clear up in time. "Everyone has accepted," Tamar overheard her tell her husband. "We can't cancel."

Now she stood across Alice's bed from Tamar. "Miss Darnell, you'll have to sing in her place."

"I?" The young woman's hand flew to her throat. "Mrs. Gregory, that is impossible."

"Of course it's not." With unexpected briskness, the older woman inquired, "I don't suppose you have an evening dress?"

Tamar shook her head and hope leaped into her eyes. Reprieved!

"No matter, you'll wear one of mine. I have a little black gown that will be marvelous with your hair; I've never worn it." She shepherded her unwilling singer into her own large room, ignoring Tamar's protests. In less than five minutes, the floating black dress settled over Tamar as if it had been created for her. Even Mrs. Gregory couldn't hide her surprise at the difference in Tamar's appearance. "Why, Miss Darnell, you're striking." She snatched the pins from Tamar's hair so that it cascaded like bright silk down her back. "There. Wear it so." She pushed a button and when a maid appeared, she ordered, "Flowers, from the conservatory, for her hair."

Tamar gave up trying to argue and submitted when the maid expertly tucked a gorgeous white flower in her hair. "But what shall I sing?"

"Anything." Mrs. Gregory waved away the obstacle and smiled. "I'll send a maid for you when we're ready."

Inspiration caused the new star to say, "I'll wait in the upper hall." It would give a clear view of the larger hall below. If an enemy came, Tamar would vanish to her own room. Her bags were already packed for her departure the next morning.

Hidden by openwork screens and a multitude of greenery, Tamar scanned the faces below. She slipped back to Alice's bedside and found the little girl asleep. Two tears still glistened on her cheeks; her birthday party had not turned out as she had hoped. Tenderness filled Tamar. *If I had a beautiful child like this one, or like Donald and Dora, I'd appreciate them, not go off seeking my own pleasure.* The thought dyed her white skin a lovely color and added sparkle to her eyes.

She had seen no one who might recognize her, and so she slipped back to her post in the upper hall and remained there until summoned to the drawing room.

"Alice is indisposed, poor child, so her music teacher has graciously consented to sing in her place," Mrs. Gregory announced after her guests were seated in the stylish but uncomfortable furniture.

Tamar couldn't tell if the little wave of sound meant pity for Alice or boredom. However, it set a flame of determination burning in her heart. They probably expected little; well, she would give them everything she could from the talent God had created in her.

What had the music school supervisor said? Ballads. Folk songs. Her audience's murmur of impatience blotted out her thoughts. Tamar opened her mouth and sang, golden notes that made old songs new. Once, twice, three times she thrilled to the silence that gave way to rousing applause.

A sudden movement to her far right caught her attention. A tardy guest must have just arrived. She glanced that way—and looked straight into the face of Phillip-with-two-l's.

"More, more!" the guests shouted.

She needed every ounce of the self control she possessed to give them one more song. She made herself laughingly decline to sing another, while edging toward the door. Just a few steps more and she'd be free. She reached the hall, sped toward the stairs.

An arm shot out of a small reception room and hauled her inside. Phillip must have scurried out of the drawing room by another door. Now he got her into the little room, shut the door, and leaned against it. "Well, well, the lost has been found."

"How dare you detain me?" The past months of self-reliance had increased Tamar's natural dignity. "Open that door at once or I shall scream and tell everyone here you have insulted me."

His eyelids closed until only a tiny bit of pupils showed. "I wouldn't do that if I were you, my dear." He drew himself up. "Your family has worried about you. I feel obligated to report to them your where-abouts." He twisted his lips. "Of course if you care to make my silence worth my while. . . ." He shrugged.

"You know I have no money," she accused.

"Oh, but you have something infinitely more valu-able," he told her. "Lorraine was livid that you clung to an heirloom tapestry she said was worth a fortune."

For a moment, Tamar felt faint. Never in her life had she felt more alone. Yet peace crept into her heart. Hadn't God promised never to forsake her?

"I see you understand." Phillip dropped his badger-ing and continued in a normal voice.

"I-I can't meet you here." She thought rapidly, blood pumping through her veins. "I had planned to leave here tomorrow and—"

"And slip away as you did from our wedding? Not this time. I'll pretend to leave with the others but hide in the library. Be there with the tapestry exactly thirty minutes after the last guest leaves or tomorrow I go to your brother." He opened the door a crack. "Fly, birdie, but don't forget what I said."

Tamar flew. Back in her room, she tore off her borrowed finery and yanked the flower from her hair. Dressed once more in her work garb, she took time to kneel by her bedside, asking God to make a way out for her.

Downstairs, the Gregories basked in the approval for

their unexpected and delightful solution to Alice's illness.

"She's exquisite." "I must have her for my next soiree." "Who is she?" "Where ever did you find her?" rang like music in Mrs. Gregory's ears, sweeter even than the songs Tamar had sung. Mrs. Gregory cautiously answered questions but gave little information. An idea had been planted in her social-climbing brain. Why not sponsor Miss Darnell, who had given such pleasure to her guests? Patrons of talented young persons occupied a special place in society. The thought gained impetus when George and Gilda Smith sought her out when her other guests had gone. George and Gilda were owners of the Pantages Theater, a much smaller establishment than the Grand Opera House, but one that was rising in popularity. "She has an unusual voice," they confirmed. "We'd be interested in speaking with her. Perhaps tomorrow?"

"She's due to leave but I'm sure Miss Darnell will be happy to stay an extra day." The arranged a time and the Smiths waited outside for their carriage to be brought around.

"I've never seen such an innocent face," Gilda remarked.

"Or such a pure voice. It hasn't been tortured into the falseness of those who ape their betters," her husband grunted. The carriage slowly rounded the corner.

Gilda glanced toward the shadows at the rear of the mansion. "Why—driver," she called. "Stop." Almost before the carriage halted she had clambered out. She ran toward the tall hedge.

eight

Phillip's order, "A half-hour after the last guest leaves" drummed in Tamar's ears. The certainty grew that she must escape now. He would be waiting in the library, not expecting her until the time he set. Her timing must be perfect to avoid being seen.

She flew to turn out the lights. There. If her employer came to the door, no betraying glimmer would give her away. The woman would think she had gone to bed. Once more she hid in the spot where she could see the guests leave. When the hall below lay empty, she snatched her bundle of belongings, crept down the long hall to the back stairs, and descended. Twice she hesitated when a whistle or snatch of laughter warned that the servants had begun the gigantic task of cleaning up after the party.

At last she reached a seldom-used door. It creaked so loudly when she unlocked it, she felt the noise could be heard in San Francisco across the bay. When no one came to investigate, she sighed with relief, breathed a prayer of thanks, and stepped into the night, glad for the shelter of hedges and shrubs and trees.

She reached the tallest hedge, prepared to dart from it into the street, when the sound of carriage wheels broke the stillness. She involuntarily glanced at the conveyance that rounded the corner, heard the command to stop, and realized she had been seen. In the past, fear had given her speed. Now it froze her still. She couldn't move. How much worse for Phillip to discover her out here than inside! He must have changed his plans or somehow discerned she had no intention of keeping the appointment.

"God, are you here?" she cried, feeling the world had ended.

"Yes, child—or at least one of His children is." A woman's voice, warm, rich, and comforting, reached out to the frightened girl. She instinctively turned to it, reassured, and found two arms around her. They reminded her of Mother's long ago.

"Come to the carriage."

Tamar didn't hesitate. Like a child, she stumbled along with her rescuer, felt herself pushed into the carriage, and heard a deep masculine laugh Phillip Carlin could never have imitated. "Gilda, my love, what have we here?"

"A frightened child. Drive on," the woman called. The carriage started. Tamar leaned weakly against the arm of the woman called Gilda, too tired to even wonder who these people were or where they were taking her. She only roused when the man asked, "Where do you want to go?"

She gave the address of her rooming house, knowing it safe for the night but not for long. Mrs. Gregory would be sure to contact the music school concerning

her vanished employee, especially after Phillip con-
cocted some lie. The school director had her address.

"Miss Darnell, we're from San Francisco but stay-
ing here in Oakland for the night. May we see you
first thing in the morning?" Gilda asked when they
reached Tamar's boarding house. "It's obvious you
are in some kind of trouble and need help. Just maybe
God sent us to offer it."

"I wouldn't be surprised," the man put in. "Don't
know any other reason why my wife and I ever agreed
to attend this affair."

Their invitation gave Tamar enough hope that she
was able to sleep. She woke at first light and lay
wondering what was ahead of her. Had it all been a
dream, the kind woman who proclaimed herself to be
a child of God? No, for if she had been dreaming,
she'd be in her room at the Gregories' instead of here
at the rooming house. Tamar sprang up, packed
everything she owned, and wrote a quick note to her
landlady. She explained she'd be changing jobs and
left a bit of money for the woman's kindness. Regardless of what Gilda and her husband said, Tamar could
no longer stay where she was.

The carriage came just as she finished her note, and
she hastened down, glad for the early hour that kept
anyone from seeing her. Gilda and her husband, who
said his name was George Smith, proved to be a
gentle pair. Each no more than five foot six inches tall,
George topped his wife's 130 pounds by another
thirty. Thinning brown hair above his round face

matched his kind brown eyes. Tamar judged him to be about forty, perhaps five years older than his wife.

Gilda's blonde hair towered in improbable curls, but her brown eyes showed compassion and trustworthiness, and her wide smile warmed Tamar's frightened heart. They took Tamar to a quiet hotel with an even quieter private dining room, waited until a substantial breakfast arrived, and then George said, "Let's bow our head in thanks."

Tamar wondered if she could swallow past the thankfulness in her throat, but gradually relaxed and found herself hungry. "I didn't eat dinner last night," she confessed. "Mrs. Gregory had just told me I had to sing."

George looked astonished. "With a voice like that, you need never dread singing, young lady." He laid his fork down and continued. "God has given you an instrument to use for good in this bad old world."

"I wasn't afraid of singing," Tamar told them. "I just didn't want to be recognized. My name isn't really Joy Darnell, but—"

"It doesn't matter and if we don't know, we can't tell." Gilda beamed until laugh lines crinkled around her eyes. "Do you have anyone who has claim to you, child? When I saw you huddled by the hedge it gave me a turn, all white-faced and scared as you were."

"Someone there did recognize me. He threatened to expose me. I've done nothing criminal and I'm eighteen years old—but there will be unpleasantness if certain persons know where I am."

"Joy, you don't mind if we call you that, do you?" When Tamar shook her head, Gilda said, "George and I own the Pantages Theatre in San Francisco. How would you like to sing for us there?'

"Why, I don't know." Tamar thought of how her family had often regarded theaters with suspicion, carefully choosing only the finest entertainment when they honored even the Grand Opera House with their presence.

"We don't have anything that would offend you," George quietly said as if he could read her mind. "Our performers are ladies and gentlemen. They dress so and conduct themselves so. The Pantages will never risk its reputation by using bawdy or common acts."

"For some time we've been wanting a soloist to sing just the kind of thing you did last night." Gilda warmed to her subject. "We've also had requests for hymns. If you feel you can work with us, we'll give you three numbers: a ballad or folk tune, something fairly light from the classics, then a hymn for your closing song." She looked wistful. "I used to sing some but my real talent is with the piano, accompanying others.

"What if I'm recognized?" Tamar voiced her greatest fear.

"Why should you be?" Gilda's eyes opened wide. "George and I talked it over and if you choose to sing at the Pantages we'd like to bill you as "The Mystery Lady." Patrons will be charmed with the idea. We've even discussed costuming. You'll wear frothy dresses, usually black or white. Mantillas will cover your hair and if you like, most of your face."

"I'd have to find somewhere to live." Tamar felt herself weakening.

"Our home is no Gregory mansion, but it's clean, comfortable, and you'd be guarded well," George promised with a steady light in his eyes. "We hate living in hotels so we purchased a comfortable dwelling that's spacious but not fancy."

Gilda patted Tamar's hand. "If you need references, we'll be happy to have you speak with our banker and minister."

Tamar made up her mind. "If you really believe I can do it, I'll try. The only references I need are already here. You love the same Lord I do." She held a hand out to each of them. "I believe He sent you when I needed help desperately."

She slipped into her new life without much notice, although from her first appearance, the Pantages Theatre rang with applause. True to their word, the Smiths whisked her in and out for rehearsals and performances; even the rest of the cast had no opportunity to form any kind of intimacy with her. Tamar had long since told the Smiths that she had run away from a loveless, arranged marriage. She suspected they knew exactly who she really was, but George and Gilda called her Joy and left it at that. Their modest house became her home, and Tamar felt like their adopted daughter. Her quiet manner and warm smile endeared her to her fellow performers, especially when she never tried to take the limelight. The portion of her face exposed below the mantilla was left in shadows by the carefully placed lighting. Secure in her anonymity, Tamar poured her golden voice out in songs that tugged at hearts. Her closing hymn always brought a reverent silence before the applause.

One night an enterprising reporter from San Francisco's largest newspaper slipped into the gallery and slumped to his seat. How could he get a decent story from a theater that refused the more risque entertainment presented in others? When George Smith introduced the next act as, "Our own Mystery Lady" the reporter snorted. The mystery would be if she could carry a tune in a teacup, although the orchestra and previous numbers had been amazingly better than he had anticipated.

Into his bored ears came the trill of bird song, wild flowers, sunrises. He jerked upright and leaned forward, entranced. "Jove, what a voice!" His mind raced with phrases to use in his column, none of them doing justice to the singer. When the final notes of her closing number died away, he leaped to his feet and made his way forward. George Smith stopped him before he could mount the steps to the stage.

"Please, I'd like to interview your singer—the Mystery Lady," the reporter pleaded.

George's short stature could still be imposing when he chose. "I'm sorry, sir, but she grants no interviews."

"Preposterous! Any woman who sings like that

needs to be heard."

"She can be heard. Here. Goodnight, sir." George crossed his arms and barred the way. He couldn't still the reporter's voice, however. The next day the popular columnist's regular offering carried the banner headline:

WHO IS THE MYSTERY LADY?

The article that followed included the fact that George and Gilda's new singer at the Pantages Theatre permitted no interviews.

The wily reporter closed with the tantalizing comment, "If I were billing anyone with such a voice, it would not be as a Mystery Lady, but as an Unknown Angel. This seasoned reporter has heard the finest visiting singers and few can compare with her pure voice. She has the ability to evoke memories of home, love, and yes, of God."

Veronica Rhys read the paper and lifted an eyebrow. "Hmm." She glanced at Gordon, deep in the business section of the newspaper. "Listen to this, will you?" She read the column aloud. "Gordon, why don't we go hear this so-called Unknown Angel?"

Mind still busy with other affairs, Gordon's gray glance showed his abstraction. "Probably more a fallen angel, I'd say. Isn't the Pantages a second rate establishment?"

"It's perfectly respectable and I understand that it's far above others of its ilk. Will you take me tomorrow night?"

"If you wish." Gordon absently turned a page. His fingers stilled and a crease formed in his forehead. "Veronica, read that again, please."

With a resigned sigh born of long experience with her often preoccupied brother, she repeated the words for him. This time his eyes glowed. She finished with, "I know this writer. Anyone who can wrest such praise from his cynical pen has to be good."

"I'll get tickets this morning," he promised.

To Gordon's chagrin, he came home from work empty-handed. "Everyone in San Francisco must have read that column," he complained. "The earliest I could get seats is Friday." He didn't add that all during his workday the thought of this Unknown Angel, as the reporter dubbed her, had intruded. For weeks and months he had sought Tamar O'Donnell. Even Hood, the human ferret, had lost the trail at the Wilsons'. The young attorney's anger burned at the way Tamar had been driven from her work by the drunken Edgar. Joy Darnell, as she had called herself, evidently had won the love and respect of the other servants. Not one had anything but praise for her and contempt for Edgar. Yet when Hood asked for an address, they clammed up.

"Clever, they are," Hood reported with a sardonic grin that changed his bland face. "One and all responded, 'I really couldn't say, sir,' leaving me to decide whether they couldn't say out of ignorance— or loyalty to Tamar."

Carlos was more haggard than ever when he learned

of the indignity his sister had suffered at the Wilsons'. "She has to be somewhere," Gordon insisted. "I wouldn't worry too much. It's obvious from the Wilson fiasco that she inspires friendship among the staff and that gives her protection."

"Protection her own brother didn't give," Carlos groaned. "Well, don't spare any expense."

Now Gordon sat and wondered. Should he mention to Carlos his niggling suspicion that this singer might be Tamar? He shook his head. If the singer were not Tamar, Carlos would receive another crushing blow. Better to see and hear her and attempt to get information the reporter had missed.

Friday evening the Pantages overflowed. The Standing Room Only sign came down with dozens of irate patrons left waiting. George and Gilda alternately rejoiced and exchanged looks of trepidation. Even high box office receipts wouldn't compensate for the loss of the girl who had taken a daughter's place, should she be recognized.

Perhaps in anticipation of hearing a new and highly lauded singer, the audience had never been more responsive. In turn, every performer sparkled. No smutty stories or suggestive acts. Just good harmony, stirring melodies, and genuinely funny exchanges between the comediennes. Then a figure swathed in a cloudy white dress and matching mantilla slowly walked to the front of the stage. A single red rose, clasped in her hand, provided color.

Gordon strained his eyes to see her shadowed face

and gasped when the first notes of Stephen Foster's beautiful ballad, "My Old Kentucky Home" rang throughout the hall. He felt Veronica stir beside him, but he was too mesmerized by the singer to glance at his sister. His face flushed when he remembered how he had classified her as a probable fallen angel. No one on earth could sing like that unless she possessed a soul clean before God.

A second song followed. Gordon closed his eyes and let the lilt of an Irish melody wash over him. But when the Unknown Angel sang the opening lines of John Newton's heartfelt cry of God's forgiveness, Gordon shivered. "Amazing grace, how sweet the sound, That saved a wretch like me! I once was lost but now am found, Was blind but now I see."

Her every word breathed her knowledge of the song's truth, and jaded San Francisco heard the message of salvation as effectively as ever preached from the pulpit. When she reached the final stanza, she opened her arms, and hundreds of voices joined in: "When we've been there ten thousand years, Bright shining as the sun, We've no less days to sing God's praise, Then when we first begun."

The audience rose for its applause. Gordon caught the satisfied smile on Veronica's lips and whispered in her ear, "Quick, the stage door!" They reached the street just in time to see a dark-cloaked figure climb into a closed carriage that drove quickly away.

"Well?" Veronica turned to her brother.

"No person here tonight can ever again plead ignorance of God's love," Gordon told her.

"I wonder who she really is and why she uses no stage name," Veronica speculated on the way home. "The way they keep her face in shadow—perhaps she is badly scarred."

Or wishes to remain incognita, Gordon's heart replied, but he stifled the words. Not even his sister must know what had become certainty from the moment he heard the Mystery Lady sing. The Unknown Angel was Tamar O'Donnell.

Now he faced a new dilemma, the worst conflict of interests he'd ever encountered. Allegiance to his client Carlos waned, while loyalty for Tamar grew out of nowhere. How could he expose her identity and have her hounded by Phillip Carlin again? His code of ethics required him to give his best to those who hired him, but he would not be part of any plot that might result in Tamar's unhappiness.

Torn by conflicting emotions, Gordon slept little that night. The next morning he called for Hood, explained the problem, and ordered him to quietly observe the Unknown Angel. He was to tell no one except Gordon what he discovered.

"Do you think she's the one?" Hood cut to the heart of it.

"If she is, I'm not sure what we'll do about it."

Hood smiled, went on his way, and came back undaunted but rebuffed. "There's better security around her than in most prisons," he cheerfully said. Gordon knew that the tougher the case, the better his secretary-turned-sleuth liked it. Hood continued, "She's delivered to the Pantages, watched like sunflowers watch for the sun, protected by the Smiths and a troupe who are strangely averse to answering questions. Every time a performance ends, she is smuggled out and away." He laughed ruefully. "I've tried three times to follow the closed carriage and three times a skillful driver has outwitted me by turning and doubling back. He ends up on busy Market Street and ostentatiously stops as if the occupants had all the time in the world before going home. But when I managed to look inside, the carriage was empty. Somehow they always manage to get out without me seeing."

"They?"

"Mrs. Smith is always with the singer."

"Keep trying." Gordon told him. "I'll approach it another way." He went to the minister of a leading cathedral and suggested that he ask the new singer to perform. His idea fell on closed ears.

"I'd as soon ask the devil himself to sing in my church as some dance hall girl," the man exploded. All Gordon's explanations only increased the minister's frown. "The theater and all who are in it are doomed to eternal punishment," the man proclaimed. "Furthermore, this—this *person's* daring to sing hymns to a trashy bunch of gawpers is blasphemy!"

Gordon subsided and marched out, then tried a new tack. Through business connections and a professed interest in the Pantages—which had certainly become real—he succeeded in meeting George Smith at a pre-arranged luncheon with a friend. George's steady gaze and kindly eyes impressed Gordon. When the mutual friend was conveniently called away, through assistance from Hood, Gordon sat on chatting. He openly expressed his appreciation that the Pantages now had someone who would bring the Gospel through song. He said nothing of wanting to meet the singer—then. Instead, he dwelled on his relationship to the Lord and how much San Francisco needed the Gospel. The city's wickedness had never been completely stamped out by the earlier vigilantes.

A few nights later, Gordon introduced Veronica to George and Gilda. The women eyed each other—one, a Nob Hill leader who had worked hard to get there; the other, a woman whose goodness couldn't be hidden by her mass of blonde hair. Both smiled and an unlikely friendship began.

nine

"Joy, we've met a nice man and his sister," Gilda said on the way home from the theater. "They're real Christians." She sounded wistful. "I'd like to invite them to our home."

"Who are they?"

"Their name is Rhys, Gordon and his sister Veronica. They may live in a mansion but they don't show it. I didn't find a trace of snobbery when George introduced us."

Tamar stretched. "Bring on your paragons. I've never heard of them before, so they can't recognize me. Oh, but how are you going to account for me living with you? Do they know I'm your singer?"

"I don't think so. We'll just say you're a dear friend who is stopping with us for awhile. It's all true, except we hope it will be for a long, long while."

"I thank God every day for you," Tamar whispered. "You bring the good Samaritan story alive."

A few days later the Rhyses arrived at the Smiths' more modest home. Their good breeding hid any possible surprise at the presence of a young, beautiful girl in the home, although Tamar saw a look of deep respect and admiration in Gordon's gray eyes and a

more thoughtful consideration in his sister's. A
simple but delicious luncheon, a wide range of dis-
cussion topics, and a friendly disagreement about
politics provided an excellent background for getting
to know one another. By professing honest interest in
rare books, Gordon maneuvered the little group into
the library. An open piano stood in one corner.

"Won't you play for us, Mrs. Smith?" he politely
asked. He laughed and added, "Does someone sing?"

"We all do," Gilda told him. Her brown eyes
danced. "How about you?"

"I'm a better listener than musician but I'll hum
along if you like."

Tamar took care to control her range and volume by
lowering her voice to blend with the others. The
Rhyses left, declaring it a happy afternoon, and
cordially inviting the Smiths to call. By mid-March
a friendly relationship had grown up between the
families. Sometimes George teased Tamar about the
multitude of flowers that came with Gordon's card.
Gilda always shushed him. "He's a nice man. Why
shouldn't he admire our Joy?"

Although Gordon looked nothing like her father,
Tamar often found depths in him, consideration and
interest, that reminded her of her precious parent.
When she admitted to herself Father would like him,
she blushed. Every time she saw him—and the times
became increasingly frequent—she liked him more.
She respected his devotion to his older sister and his

dedication to God. She listened to what others said of
him and avidly read newspaper reports of his court
cases, secretly rejoicing when he won justice and
reprieve for those falsely accused. He had long since
told her and the Smiths that he never represented any
person whose innocence he doubted.

Tamar continued to gain popularity as the Unknown Angel and banked most of her generous
salary. The Smiths went on protecting her, but
Gordon had crept into the inner circle of friendship
and often escorted her here and there, although never
to the Pantages. She secretly trembled and wondered
that a man as wonderful as he could be interested in
an unknown girl named Joy Darnell. In the short
weeks of their friendship, Tamar had become convinced of his worth. She might sway like a palm tree,
bent by the storms of life; Gordon stood strong, an oak
of a Welshman with his stocky body, sandy hair, and
gray eyes.

The one bitter drop in her filling cup of happiness
was a change in Veronica's attitude. She remained
courteous, even warm, yet Tamar saw a shadow of
doubt in the eyes that resembled Gordon's. Once
Gordon had admitted to a long line of proper and rigid
ancestors, spotless and stern; did Veronica feel Joy
Darnell couldn't live up to her brother's heritage?

Tamar's sensitive spirit shrank from what she per-
ceived as class-consciousness. When some distant
relatives visited the Rhyses while she was present, the

feeling grew. Coming lightly downstairs to meet Gordon, she overheard one of the pinched-lips cousins inquire, "Who is the young woman with the heathenish hair, dyed, of course. Tell me, Gordon surely isn't interested in *her*?"

Tamar backed away, face as fiery as her hair. A little balm soothed her heart when Veronica answered, "She's a dear friend—of us both," and turned the subject. Tamar fled to a nearby powder room, cooled her hot face, summoned up the O'Donnell dignity, and boldly marched into the lions' den. In this case, the cats' slanted gaze slid away from her when she returned their haughty stares.

"Just like Carlos," she muttered to herself when she got home. "Stiff-necked, convinced God created them a little more in His image than other mortals." The crisp indictment chased away some of her troubled thoughts.

Gordon was experiencing troubles of his own. They started when Veronica accusingly said, "Do you know Joy Darnell is really the Unknown Angel of the Pantages?" She quivered indignantly.

"So?" Her brother raised sandy brows in the way that infuriated her.

"So you've been escorting her."

"And plan to continue as much as she will allow." He threw the gauntlet of challenge squarely into her lap. "If Ta-Joy can ever care for me the way I do her, she's going to be Mrs. Gordon Rhys."

Veronica gasped as if he'd thrown ice water into her face. "You can't mean it! She's a nice enough little thing and does have a remarkable voice, but think of your position."

Gordon's knowledge of his sister tempered the quick retort that rose to his lips. Only too well did he know how hard she had worked to help him achieve popularity. "My dear, there are several things you don't know about Miss Darnell, ones I am not at liberty to share. But can't you see she is refined and far above the other Nob Hill women?"

"I thought her so until she set her cap for you." Veronica's eyes filled with misery.

"She didn't." Gordon's lips firmed into a straight line. "She's no adventuress, far from it. Veronica, I'm going to ask you to trust me. One day you will thank God for your sister-in-law, God willing. We don't want harsh words and condemnation now, for later they will turn to regret for judgments made without having all the facts." He laughed. "Besides, the lady in question may not have me."

His sister did a complete turnabout. "She's a fool if she won't." The next moment she looked sheepish. "Well, you've chased enough women, so I suppose I can take your word. You're old enough to know what you're doing. I just wish you could tell me what the mystery is."

"I do, too," Gordon said soberly. "But I can't—at least, not yet." He crossed to where she sat and rumpled her carefully brushed hair. "Thanks, old gal."

"You needn't throw my age in my face." But Veronica's smile told him she understood, as she had always done.

Each day, Gordon thought he would confess his love to Tamar-Joy. Each day he refrained. His legal mind told him to wait; they hadn't known each other long, although throughout his search for her, he felt he had come to know her well. He also continued to struggle with divided loyalties. Soon he must either betray her whereabouts to Carlos or drop the case. Slowly a solution came to him, a daring plan. What if he proposed and once she accepted him, presented the O'Donnells with both the runaway and her fiancé? His hopes were raised by the gladness in her dark eyes whenever she saw him, and the idea grew to determination. Tomorrow he would call for her, drive to a secluded spot in a park, and ask her to be his wife.

"Good thing, too," he admitted aloud. "I've been so concerned about her it's hard to concentrate." He stretched. Strange. Now that he'd made up his mind, he felt fresher and better able to tackle his job than he'd been in months. He fell to and buried himself deep in an upcoming case, only to be interrupted by Hood, who ushered in a raging Carlos O'Donnell.

"Why haven't you told me Tamar is the singer at the Pantages—the Unknown Angel?" he hissed.

"How did you find out?" Gordon, who usually kept

secrets safe behind his padlocked lips, blurted out the worst thing he could say.

Carlos clenched his fists. "When you continued to report no success, I hired a private detective." His mouth twisted into a sneer. "He traced 'Joy Darnell' back to the music school and the Gregories of Oakland, who are twittering about the wonderful success of their so-called protégé—something you should have done. How long have you known?"

Gordon regained control; his gray eyes turned glacial. "I still don't know for certain, although I suspected it when I heard her sing."

"You dared withhold information? I'll have you up for unethical practice," Carlos threatened.

"Have you seen her?"

"I have—at the Pantages Theatre where she flaunts herself before the common herd."

Gordon bounced up from behind his desk. "You prate to me of being unethical? What about your guilt, your trying to marry her to Carlin? I suppose, if she returns to your home, you'll attempt to arrange another marriage for her."

"Who are you to question me?" Carlos turned livid.

"The man who is going to marry Tamar O'Donnell."

Carlos sank into a chair, speechless. He raised a shaking hand and finally said, "You?"

Gordon could almost see the older man's brain working in shrewd consideration of the information hurled at him. If Tamar married San Francisco's most popular young attorney, it would solve her problems as well as Carlos and Lorraine's. Resignation and an attempt at restoring his dignity made Carlos's voice stiff. "I wish you well, Rhys. She is far too spirited to make a good wife, but—" He shrugged and surprised Gordon with his sudden laugh. "Perhaps you're the one who can gentle her. As for the other, I hope you will forget it."

Gordon's fair nature came to his aid. "I've fought with this problem for days and I understand your viewpoint. Now if you'll excuse me, I've waited far too long to settle things with your sister." He reached for his hat and started toward the door.

"I hope you aren't too late." Carlos's voice stopped him as effectively as a bullet. Gordon whipped around. A genuine look of anxiety had settled on his client's face. It reflected in what he said. "I was so angry with Tamar, I told her I'd be back in an hour to pick her up with her belongings. She didn't argue but I saw the way she looked at that funny little owner and his wife. I hope she's still there."

Cold fear swept over Gordon. "So do I." He rushed out, closely followed by Carlos who shouted he must go along. Gordon didn't have time to argue.

Every inch of the way to the Pantages the two men leaned forward, as if doing so would push the O'Donnell carriage faster. The driver stopped abruptly in front of the theater. To Gordon's horror, a large sign had been nailed across the door. It read:

CLOSED UNTIL FURTHER NOTICE

"Quickly," he commanded. "To the Smiths'." He shouted the address and held tightly to the seat when the carriage lurched around corners and raced up streets. On arrival, Gordon sprang to the ground. "Better let me go first." He ran up to the front door that had opened for him in welcome so often before. Now it stayed forbiddingly shut, even when he pounded. Good heavens, the Smiths and Tamar couldn't have vanished in such a short time, could they? He beat until his knuckles ached and only stopped when footsteps sounded behind him.

"George, where is she?" He seized the shorter man in strong hands, noting the anger and disillusionment in his eyes.

"Safe." George tore himself free and cast an unfriendly look at Carlos, who had joined them. "No thanks to either of you."

"You don't understand," Gordon told him. "I love her and it's all right with Mr. O'Donnell and—"

"Fine way to show it." George skirted the two and headed for the house. "He comes bursting into a rehearsal, babbling and accusing. Joy just stands there with her sweet white face and big dark eyes while he tells her he's had a lawyer after her and she's got to do what he says. She gasps and grabs at her throat. 'What lawyer?' she shoots back. When he yells, 'Rhys' she looks sick and turns even whiter."

"He's her brother, George." Gordon tried to turn

the tide.

"Think I don't know that? My wife and I rescued her in Oakland when that sniveling Carlin showed up at the Gregories'." The Pantages' owner drew himself up until he looked far taller than his height. "We took her in and cared for her like the child we never had, loved her, too, more than life." He blinked and swallowed hard. "We put San Francisco at her feet, at least those who are decent and enjoy her singing. Now—" He spread his hands. "She's gone."

"Where?" Gordon wanted to shake him. "Don't you understand? I was on my way to ask her to marry me! And I *didn't betray her*. O'Donnell got tired of getting no results and hired a private detective who somehow did what my man couldn't."

A wide range of emotions played on George's round face. Disbelief, scorn, growing acceptance, pity. "It's too bad she doesn't know that."

"She will." Gordon grimly set his jaw in the look lying witnesses dreaded. "If it takes the rest of my life, I'll find her and when I do, only God Himself will ever take her away from me—if she'll forgive my not speaking sooner."

"Then we'd better hurry!" George became an ally. "Joy—I'll always think of her by that name—is leaving for the East Coast on the next train out of Oakland. A boat captain friend took her and Gilda across the Bay." His accusing gaze cut deep into Gordon. "Seemed better that way then having her start her journey here where she could be traced." He answered the unspoken questions that hung in the air. "We figured you'd show up so I came back to stall for time. Confound it, O'Donnell, how could you treat that beautiful sister of yours in such a way?"

A flush rose under Carlos's dark skin. "I've asked myself that a hundred times." He stared out the window and in spite of the perilous situation, Gordon felt sorry for him. All he said, however, was, "Can't we go faster?"

It took time to reach Oakland, more time to get to the railway station. When they did, a lone, blonde-haired woman stood weeping beside empty tracks, with her face turned east.

"She's gone?" George put his arms around her shoulders.

"Yes." Gilda's red-rimmed eyes and swollen face showed the cost of Tamar's leaving. George quickly explained what had happened.

"When's the next train?" Gordon demanded.

"I don't know. It won't do any good, anyway," Gilda said in a flat voice. "Joy doesn't even know where she's going. She laughed, a hurting little laugh, and said it didn't matter. We can't do anything until we hear from her. She promised she would let me know where she goes."

"I still think I should go," Gordon insisted. Yet those long rails that dwindled into the distance, calling him to follow, held no clue to what lay in

Tamar's mind. In addition, his work schedule and sense of duty tugged heavily at him. Finally, he and Carlos reluctantly agreed the best thing was to return to San Francisco and wait for a message.

From the frail shelter of neatly stacked boxes a short distance away, Tamar watched them go. After Gilda saw her on the train and unwillingly left her, Tamar sank into a ball of helpless misery, but only for a few moments. Then her O'Donnell strength and grand-mother's pluck jerked her upright. More important, a whisper in her heart grew more insistent and pound-ed in her brain that there must be some explanation for what Carlos had told her. Gordon Rhys, with his steady gray eyes, could not be untrue! If she ran away now, she would never know—and she must. The scene at the Pantages had done more than humiliate her. It had also opened the door to the knowledge that she loved Gordon. Otherwise, the pain could never be so intense, her disappointment in him so great.

"I'll go straight to him and find out for myself," she decided. The train gave a warning whistle and Tamar sprang to her feet. Yet even as she started toward the station, she hesitated. If Carlos became unpleasant, wouldn't it affect her new friends?

She instinctively turned the other way, going from car to car until she had put a goodly distance between herself and Gilda. Snatching up the faithful woven bag she had so hastily stuffed with the tapestry and a

few clothes, she bided her time. Just as the warning
whistle sounded again, she slipped off, shielded by a
group of laughing passengers who stood nearby. She
bowed her head and shrank among them, then followed until they began to disperse. With a frantic
prayer, Tamar darted to the boxes, knowing she must
get away before someone came to move them. Not
yet, for Gilda still stood looking east.

Tamar turned and watched the train disappear from
sight. When she finally looked back, three men had
joined Gilda. Tamar crouched lower, her body turned
to ice. George. Carlos. Gordon. *Why?* Had her
brother convinced the others they must turn her over
to him? She searched for another explanation and
found none, then ventured a peep. Now Gilda was
saying something and shaking her head. Gordon
moved impatiently, and she saw the sun glint on his
bare, sandy head. He pointed down the tracks, then
took a step toward the station. Did he mean to go after
her?

No, for Gilda spoke again. Oh, God, had she been
wrong about the Smiths? The little group appeared to
be arguing, but after a short time, they walked away
together without a backward glance. Tamar wanted
to run after them, to plead with Carlos for the truth and
freedom, to look into the Smiths' kindly eyes and find
the faithfulness she had trusted in for all these weeks.
Her legs wouldn't move. Gordon had linked arms
with Carlos, and the quartet gradually became blurred

by distance and tears. So it was true. All Gordon
Rhys ever wanted from her was to confirm her real
identity. Well, now he knew. So would the world.
What would Veronica and all the proud Rhys relatives say? That Gordon got what he deserved for
dallying with anyone who had heathenish hair, dyed,
of course?

ten

Again, Tamar began a new life. She had tried to be a children's companion, with disastrous results. Her career as the Unknown Angel had ended abruptly. She carefully considered her narrowing choices and at last decided to simply let God order her future. For the present, the earnings from the Pantages would keep her for a long time. She decided to remain in Oakland. Few knew her there, and she would avoid those who did. To that end, she stayed away from the fine stores patronized by the rich and made her purchases in smaller, less pretentious establishments. She sought out the simplest accommodations and disclosed nothing of her past. She also gave up the name Joy Darnell and signed herself J. Donald to prevent discovery.

The lonely life on which she had embarked offered security and little else. Some contentment came from spring itself, but even though Oakland was a beautiful city, she missed San Francisco. Did she dare return? Could she lose herself in the crowds and yet be in the city she loved?

One morning she awakened from a dream in which Gordon Rhys had stretched out pleading arms. His gray eyes looked sad and she heard him whisper,

"Come back, Tamar." When she opened her eyes and realized where she was, she remembered he had said "Tamar," not "Joy." All day she was distracted by the question of whether she had been betrayed by the man she had grown to love. By nightfall, she decided she would go back to San Francisco, in spite of the possible risk. She had successfully hidden in Oakland crowds; in San Francisco she could catch glimpses of Gordon from some obscure spot, and with her plain garb and shaded face, he'd never know. An obsession took hold of her—that just seeing him would in some way let her know if he truly had been false.

As much as she wanted to return to her first San Francisco landlady, Tamar knew it would never do. Neither could she contact George and Gilda Smith when they might be influenced by Carlos. So again she sought and found the plainest of lodgings, smiled, and kept her own counsel. "J. Donald" slipped back into the pool of San Francisco humanity without a ripple.

Unwilling to do anything to call attention to herself, she carefully portioned her money so it would last the longest possible time. The feeling persisted that God would lead when the time came. In the meanwhile, what need had she of fancy clothing and fripperies?

Gradually, the lonely girl set aside her troubles and became interested in life around her. The city buzzed with excitement over the coming of the Metropolitan Opera Company from New York to perform in the Grand Opera House. From Market Street to Telegraph Hill, stories ran rampant, stories of the luxurious cars in which the stars traveled with costumes and scenery, of the European tours where the stars' fame had shone bright, and of the display of jewelry to be worn by patrons. The Palace Hotel preened itself for their elegant rooms near to the opera house, thereby garnering most of the visiting singers. Flowers filled the Hotel, and the Palace's usual excellent service became even better.

The second piece of news that April of 1906 concerned the terrible fact that Italy's Mt. Vesuvius had roused from dormancy and begun to shake itself into action. San Francisco with its many Italians sent aid to the fleeing homeless in Naples. Several other towns were also in danger, just as in the days of Pompeii.

"How can people be so stupid as to live near an active volcano?" many asked, even while gathering funds.

Tamar had long since managed to purchase entrance to the opera *Carmen*, scheduled for April 17. When the night came, she hurried into an obscure corner, peered at the flashing array of jewels, and noted with a twisted smile how Phillip-with-two-l's Carlin occupied a prominent box with a jeweled dowager and a haughty ash blond woman. Tamar breathed a little prayer of thanks. But for the grace of God, she would be Tamar Carlin now, bound forever to a selfish, domineering man.

The Grand Opera House had been garlanded with

blossoms and greenery. Roses perfumed the air. Tamar forgot Phillip Carlin and lost herself in the performance.

Not until intermission did Tamar catch sight of Gordon Rhys, aisles away. Her heart fluttered when his keen eyes lit up and he half rose. Had he seen her? She shrank back; hopefully, if he looked her way again he would think he'd been mistaken. She peeped around the shelter of a broad-backed man and saw a woman had clutched Gordon's arm and motioned him to be seated again. Tamar had to know who she was. She waited until Gordon turned his gaze toward the stage where the performance had resumed, then leaned sideways until she could see the woman. "Veronica!" A sigh of relief escaped her.

"Shhh," the heavy-set man beside her admonished.

Tamar obediently subsided, but although Enrico Caruso, the great Italian tenor, sang as never before, only half of Tamar's attention stayed with him. She must leave before the performance ended, but how? She frantically considered ways to escape and rejected them all. If she feigned illness, it would cause a stir and those gray eyes would see it. Finally, she decided her best plan lay in mingling with the crowd. Gordon and Veronica would need time to leave their seats and reach her. She would be inconspicuous among the crowd.

A silent prayer for help shot skyward. During the standing ovation, she slipped from her place, and ignoring the black looks she received when she stumbled over feet, she reached the door. She dared not use a public conveyance whose driver might remember her, and so despite the miles that lay between her and her boarding place, she darted away from the Grand Opera House into the night.

Lower lip caught between her teeth, haunted by fear but trusting in the Lord, Tamar set out on the most frightening walk of her life. Each time a dog or cat separated itself from the shadows, she cringed. Most of the streets were lighted, yet here and there she passed dark alleys where danger might hide.

Hours later she reached the haven of her sparsely furnished room. Midnight had come and gone. Exhausted from her trek, heartsick at the vivid thrust of emotion she had felt when she saw Gordon, Tamar listlessly undressed, got into her nightgown, and fell into bed. She wondered why life had to be so hard and if it would ever get better.

The moment Gordon saw Tamar across the flower-filled opera house, hope revived in his heart. Until now, he, Carlos, and Hood had made no progress toward finding the whereabouts of the Unknown Angel. No trace of her remained. Gordon lost weight and took little care of himself. Veronica stormed, Hood encouraged, to no avail. Somewhere the woman he loved and had hoped to marry wandered the country friendless, believing he had betrayed her. Only the necessity of diligence in his job kept him from total despair.

"Sit down, Gordon, it's beginning again." Veronica's low reprimand brought him back to the present. "Whatever is the matter with you?"

Before the house lights dimmed, Gordon looked across the space separating them from Tamar. To his amazement, she appeared to have vanished. Surely she couldn't have seen him and fled so soon! He strained his eyes and discerned a bit of black clothing just behind a moon-faced man. His legal mind tackled the problem. If she hadn't seen him, he needn't worry. If she had, she couldn't get out without attracting attention. He settled back in his chair for the rest of the performance and heard as little of it as Tamar had. The instant it ended, he leaped to his feet. "I'll be back," he told his amazed sister.

It took Herculean effort to get through the milling crowd. "Well, really, I never saw such a rude man," followed him when he dodged between two society women.

Gordon had marked well the exact location where Tamar sat and lunged toward it—only to find a gesticulating man who beamed and pounded a friend on his back.

"Did you see a young lady?" Gordon interrupted.

"Did you lose one?" The man and his companion roared with laughter. "Plenty more young ladies. Take your pick." He waved and went into fresh gales of laughter.

Gordon turned away. He crowded through droves of people and finally reached the door. Private carriages stood waiting for their owners. He questioned a few of the drivers and received only head shakes. Too many people had poured out for anyone to remember one young woman in black.

Defeated, yet strangely exhilarated that Tamar at least was in the city and not somewhere known only to God, Gordon wended his way back to Veronica.

Her sandy brows rose at his disheveled appearance. "Well, you decided to come back, did you?"

He lowered his voice, aware of curious onlookers. "She was here, Veronica. I saw Tamar." He had told her sister the girl's identity after his frantic trip to Oakland weeks before.

"Impossible! She left on the train, didn't she?"

"We thought she did. Either she never went or has come back."

"You must be mistaken, Gordon." Sympathy showed in the gray eyes so like his. "Why would she risk being seen by coming here tonight?"

"Perhaps she couldn't resist the temptation of hearing Caruso sing. You know how she loves music," he reminded and helped her into her lightweight cape.

"What will you do now?" she asked before turning to go.

"Turn San Francisco upside-down if I have to," he grimly said. "Even if she can never learn to care for me, she has to know I didn't give her away to Carlos."

Once at home on Nob Hill, they talked far into the night. Veronica's support had swung to the mysterious singer once she realized how much her brother loved Tamar and how courageously Tamar had fled from marriage with Phillip. "If she's back in the city, Hood will find her," she told Gordon, then yawned. "We'd best get to bed. It's only a few hours until daylight. Don't worry, old dear. If the good Lord wants you to find her, you will."

"I just wish I hadn't waited so long to tell her I cared." Gordon moodily stared at the wall. "All this could have been avoided. I guess I was afraid it was too soon to speak."

Veronica patted him on the shoulder and said nothing. He went to his own room but lay sleepless. Had there been reproach in the dark eyes when their fleeting gaze had met his? He tossed and turned, knowing he must sleep. Tomorrow, no, today, offered a new chance to find her. Yet his eyes persisted in popping open and he watched the pre-dawn gloom grow lighter.

Suddenly a violent lurch of his bed brought him upright. Another leap sent him to his feet, the floor beneath him rolling like ocean breakers. Priceless paintings and statuary plummeted from the walls. "God, help us! And Tamar." His fear for her was greater than for himself, as the earthquake continued its devastation.

"Gordon!" Veronica's voice rose above the screaming of the servants. He somehow managed to step into trousers, wondering if the ceiling would come down on them all before they could get outside. A minute of calm only preceded another grinding, groaning attack as the earth slid and quivered and bucked.

"*Go outside!*" Gordon bellowed. "Into the garden, away from the house." The sound of falling masonry all but drowned his voice. He raced to steady Veronica, who had struggled into a dressing gown. Together they lurched into the hall toward the head of the staircase. They skirted piles of smashed treasures, clutched one another for support, and somehow made it down the dancing staircase that threatened to buckle beneath their feet. Master, mistress, and servants gathered in the garden and clung to one another. Like a scene of horror, the streets were filled with half-dressed people under a steel-blue sky. Unlike many spring days that began with soft fog, at 5:13 in the morning this April 18th was already hot, a merciless sun beginning to rise.

"Look." Gordon pointed below them. Smoke drifted up from the south of Market Street. "Fires," he quietly added. "From overturned stoves and gas lamps." He turned from the scene. "Thank God none of us is hurt. I'll check the neighboring homes."

"Wait, Gordon." Veronica's face looked ghastly in the early morning. "The people. They're coming here."

He whipped around. Far below a steady procession of men, women, and children fled the fire and destruction surrounding them. The distant fires grew more menacing, and when the first of the refugees reached them, he panted, "Water main's broken! Can't stop the fires. God, send us rain."

Before long the lower end of Market Street lay masked by smoke and the Mission District pulsed with noise and confusion, engulfed with fire. Tall buildings became black ruins. Morning limped on, and a line of red fire serpentined up the hills toward Nob Hill. With only water from the Bay available, the best efforts proved futile. The dull boom of dynamite added to the pall over the city; buildings were being blown up to try to stop the fire.

Gordon insisted on going down to help and came back hours later, grimy and heartsick. "So many dead and hundreds injured! Chinatown was gone by noon. The North Beach Italian quarter's burned. There are refugee camps at the Presidio and in Golden Gate Park." He spread his hands wide. "I can't and won't order any of you," he told his servants, "but they need all the help they can get."

Veronica cast one look at the home she'd worked so hard to get, then set her lips in a straight line. "Will the fire reach Nob Hill?"

"Yes, but we're alive." Gordon dropped an arm around his sister's shoulders. He didn't dare add the question hovering on his lips, but knew she understood his concern for Tamar.

Veronica squared her shoulders and said, "So be it. We can at least help others."

The first night saw rich and poor, old and young alike joined in a common cause. No fires nor candles could be lit even in undamaged houses. Quickly constructed stoves made of brick stood outside, and what little cooking San Francisco did was on those. The injured moaned, the bereaved cried—and all prayed for rain that did not come.

For three days Nob Hill residents worked with Chinese, Italians, and refugees from all over the city. Gordon never passed a blanketed figure or wounded person without a quick prayer that it wouldn't be Tamar. Once he burst out to Veronica, "I could stand all the rest, losing our home and office building and possessions, if only I knew she were all right."

"You don't know that she isn't." Veronica took both his hands in hers and looked deeply into the tortured gray eyes.

"But the death toll is nearing seven hundred." Gordon groaned and pulled free. "They say three hundred thousand have lost their homes."

Veronica looked at the wrecked, wretched city and said soberly, "It's a miracle it isn't seven thousand or seventy thousand dead. Have faith, Gordon." The shine of tears softened her tired face.

"I'm trying." He brushed his hand across his eyes and left her standing there among the injured, where she'd been almost twenty-four hours a day since the earthquake.

Tamar had suffered a blow to the head in the initial tremor. Along with the rest of the city, her boarding place shook and lurched. Dazed from falling plaster, she managed to stagger from her room as great chunks of ceiling fell around her.

"Miss Donald?" her landlady's husband called.
"Gather your things quickly." His worried face
appeared at his door. "We'll have to get out if. . . ."

She was too dazed to hear the rest of his sentence.
Her fingers came away bloodstained when she touched
her aching forehead. She pressed a handkerchief to it,
remembered the water in her pitcher, and stepped
over debris until she could wet her handkerchief. She
quickly grabbed the faithful Mexican bag, checked to
be sure her tapestry lined the bottom, and hurriedly
stuffed in whatever clothes she could find, glad that
her hoard of money remained pinned inside her
garments where she kept it.

"Folks are camping in Lafayette Square," she learned
when she got outside. "We'll go there."

Tamar weaved through the next days like one in a
never-ending nightmare. With all her heart she longed
to rush to Nob Hill and find out what had happened
to Gordon Rhys, to Carlos and Veronica—even Lorraine.
How trivial and foolish her trials seemed when compared with the human misery around her! Yet duty
called. Except for a lump on her head and a slight cut
that stopped bleeding within minutes, she had come
through the inferno unscathed. Others had not. Praying for added strength and courage, she did what she
could under the direction of those more skilled than
she, dreading every new patient for fear if would be
someone she loved. She also vowed that if God
allowed her to survive the continuing threat of danger, as soon as she could leave those who needed her,

she would go to Gordon and Carlos and no longer
hide. The promise sustained her. The work she did
was the hardest and most menial she had ever done,
yet in a way it was also the most satisfying.

All around her, indomitable people spoke of rebuilding their city once the crisis was over. The spirit
of San Francisco burned like a torch of hope, bright-
ening even the darkest hours. Yet many times Tamar
cried to God, praying that her family and Gordon had
been spared, wishing passionately she could know,
yet refusing to desert her post.

And in another part of the city, Gordon experienced
the same pangs, only to a greater degree. Although
his Nob Hill residence had burned, Tamar could find
him if she chose through anyone who knew him. He
had no idea where she might be. Day and night, words
he had spoken long ago returned to haunt him. *If it
takes the rest of my life, I'll find her—and when I do,
only God Himself will ever take her away from
me. . . .*

Was that what had happened during the terrible
earthquake and fires? Had God taken Tamar? If that
were so, was life worth living?

eleven

The Nob Hill mansions had burned like gigantic torches, gobbled up by the fire that blew toward Russian and Telegraph Hills. According to rumor, Caruso had snatched an autographed picture of President Teddy Roosevelt, then hired a wagon for three hundred dollars, and driven over shattered streets to the outskirts of town; once he was on a transcontinental train out of Oakland, he swore never to return.

Cracked streets and twisted streetcar tracks served as grim reminders of the earthquake's power. Help poured in from other parts of the country, and martial law helped enforce the mayor's proclamation that looting or other criminal acts would result in death. Tens of thousands had left the city, but many more stuck it out, even singing around a rescued piano in Golden Gate Park in the evenings.

The spirit of San Francisco waxed strong and those who had lost fortunes predicted, "Our city will be stronger and more beautiful than ever. Steel-reinforced buildings will be built."

Tamar did not keep her vow. Her selfless giving to others took a toll on her body. As long as she had to keep going, she did, but when the dead had been buried and the last of the injured no longer needed her attention, the faithful helper crumpled into a heap in a Red Cross makeshift hospital.

For days she didn't know where or who she was. The few times she opened her eyes, she stared blankly at the nurse who hovered over her and demanded, "Where is Tamar?" again and again. Sometimes she called out in delirium, "The tapestry. I must have the tapestry." But when the nurses and doctor questioned her, she only mumbled and tossed.

"She worked herself nearly to death," a kindly nurse confirmed. "I never had to tell her more than once what to do."

"What's this tapestry she keeps crying for?" The gruff doctor's shaggy brows drew together.

The nurse shook her head. "No one knows. We searched the vicinity she worked in and found nothing. When we undressed her, we discovered money hidden in her gown but that's all."

"Well, we don't have time now to hunt for relatives, God knows." The weary doctor sighed. "Without having examined her at the time it happened, I'd say she's experiencing a delayed reaction to that head injury, compounded by lack of sleep and too much hard work. Keep her warm, give her all the broth she'll take, and if you're a Christian woman, pray. It's all we can do." He shook his head. "I suspect she was carrying some kind of burden before she got hurt."

He rested a toil-worn hand on Tamar's slender one where it lay on the coverlet. "Child, whatever's

troubling you, forget it." The strain around the
sleeping girl's mouth lessened just a little. "Remember, there's nothing to worry about. We're taking
good care of you." He turned abruptly. "I'll be back
this evening if I can leave the others. If there's a
change, send word immediately."

Fathoms deep in her fatigue, Tamar occasionally
heard voices but they meant nothing to her. Again
and again, she lived the horrendous days and nights
following the earthquake. In her nightmares, faces
from the past plagued her tired mind. Carlos. Lorraine.
Dick. Why, she'd forgotten her own brother in the
turmoil and now even in her dreams, she gave a
thankful prayer he'd been away at school, far from the
stench of fire and death. The memory of his smiling
eyes strengthened her. She quieted but thrashed when
Gordon Rhys's haggard face came to the front of her
thoughts. She'd never seen him so worn and worried.
Tamar, where are you? he repeated over and over
until she struggled out of the clutching shadows and
whispered brokenly, "I'm here."

The overworked doctor lifted his eyebrows when
the nurse reported his patient's mumblings. "Hmmm.
First she asked where Tamar was and now she says
'I'm here.' Unusual name. It shouldn't be hard to
trace her family." He scowled down at her pale face
surrounded by the wealth of red-gold hair. "Pity, but
that hair's going to have to be cut. Those masses are
too much for her right now." He shook his head.
"Don't cut all of it, just enough to get rid of the

weight."

"Yes, doctor." The motherly nurse waited until he finished his examination, then fetched scissors. Tress by tress, the silken hair fell to the coverlet until Tamar resembled nothing so much as a medieval page boy. Still her nervous fingers plucked at the air, and the good woman sighed. Would they find relatives in time to bring this lovely child back from the edge of death? The nurse's keen eyes and years of experience told her how slim a chance her patient had unless something drastic happened soon. With the faith born of early teaching and increased by her work, the woman bowed her head, took the restless hands in her capable ones, and prayed aloud, "Father, be with this, Thy child. For Jesus's sake, amen."

Six days after the earthquake, while smoke from the smoldering buildings still filled the air, Mayor Schmitz called a committee of leading citizens to plan how to rebuild shattered San Francisco. The United States Congress had already promised to replace or repair lost and damaged government buildings. Oakland newspapers spit out disaster news to the rest of the country, and it would become a matter of history that no one went hungry or thirsty in the aftermath of the juggernaut.

Gordon Rhys, Carlos O'Donnell, and dozens of other well-off citizens donned overalls and flannel shirts and grabbed picks and shovels. Gordon was also beset by claims and rejoiced when most insurance companies paid off on the burned properties. The daily hard work created a happy, cooperative spirit, but Gordon avoided the quickly thrown together dance platforms; instead, in the few free hours he allowed himself, he combed the city.

He and Veronica found shelter with friends whose home had been spared, although fire had crept to its doorstep before the wind shifted. Always he asked those he met, "Did you run across a girl named Tamar O'Donnell, or one called Joy Darnell?" Negative head-shakes and looks of sympathy accompanied his listeners' responses. Sometimes he wondered if she had safely fled, then reminded himself she had actually been in San Francisco the night of the seventeenth. He fought a war within, torn between wanting to let Carlos know he had seen Tamar, yet unwilling to add more misery to the other man's burden.

"Don't ask me why or how she thinks this way, but Lorraine blames me for our losing our mansion," Carlos confided in Gordon when they worked side by side on the clean up crew. No longer the Spanish grandee, the new Carlos that had risen phoenix-like from the ashes commanded more respect in overalls than he ever had before.

"You'll rebuild, won't you?"

Carlos shrugged and his white teeth gleamed in his sweaty face. "Perhaps. Only Dios knows." He relaxed his furious digging for a moment and leaned on the shovel handle. "At least I'm thankful Tamar wasn't here. I'd give my life to know she's safe somewhere, though."

"So would I." Gordon cleared his husky voice. "I still hope to find and marry her."

"I wish you well. Nothing would please me more." A shade of bitterness crossed his face. "Even Lorraine would find you acceptable." His look of understanding took any sting from his words, and he resumed work as furiously as if he alone must restore the city by the Bay.

Gordon held his tongue and continued to ask God to care for Tamar. For the first time he truly understood Paul's admonition to the Thessalonians, "Pray without ceasing."* Not only Tamar but thousands of others needed prayers, and every waking moment found Gordon drawing close to his Lord, upholding those in need. He realized how much nearer to God he had grown through all the turmoil. So had others. Grateful for life itself, many who had frantically implored God's mercy now took a stand for Him.

One particularly weary evening, Gordon turned his steps in yet another direction. He had methodically mapped out the city and planned to search it all. Only then would he accept that Tamar might be one of those hastily buried in the first wave of death. If she had died while living under an assumed name, authorities would be unable to notify her family. A dozen times he asked his question, but no one had seen her. When he reached the point of exhaustion and reluctantly turned back, knowing he must rest in order to make it through the next day, he raised his face to the

*I Thessalonians 5:17

heavens and cried, "Oh God, please! Just a word of her. That's all I ask. I have to know. If she's dead, I'll accept it and try to go on and live for You, but I can't stand this terrible uncertainty." He paused, whispered an amen, and slowly walked to his temporary home.

Three days passed and nothing changed. On the third evening when he dragged in from work, Veronica met him at the door. "They're here. Gordon, come!" She snatched his arm and literally dragged him into a small reception room off the main hall. "They just came and I haven't had time to talk with them, but maybe—"

Gordon had never heard his sister babble so. He stopped short in the doorway. "George, Gilda, you're safe!" Wrenching free from Veronica's hold, he strode across the room and shook hands with them both, noting new lines in George's round face. Gilda's blonde hair lay in simple waves instead of the high, tortured hairdo she had worn at the Pantages.

Veronica asked the question forming on Gordon's lips. "Have you heard from Tamar?"

Gordon felt the world stop for the heartbeat before the Smiths shook their heads. "Not a word, but—" Gilda broke off and dug in the large bag she carried. "We found this wrapped around an injured child in Golden Gate Park." A soiled, crumpled piece of fabric dangled from her fingers.

Gordon snatched it. His eyes burned as he fingered what had once been a scarlet, emerald, and white design. "Tamar's?" Could that be his voice, broken, filled with fear?

"Yes." Gilda's brown eyes misted with tears. "Her most cherished possession, all she had left from her parents."

George took up the story. "We'd been praying for Joy-Tamar and doing our bit in cleaning up, when we saw the child in his mother's arms, the tapestry wrapped like a blanket around him. It took some persuasion, but when the mother realized how much this meant to us, she insisted on giving it to us."

"But I found no trace of Tamar in the park," Gordon protested.

"The child's mother said a kind lady had wrapped him in the cloth while they were in Lafayette Square," Gilda explained. "Later they moved on to Golden Gate Park."

"How long ago was this?" Gordon clutched the dirty tapestry until his knuckles showed white.

"We're not sure. The poor woman had lost track of time. We tried to find out more, but we had no success." Sympathy breathed through George's words.

An odd shiver ran up Gordon's spine. "When did you get the tapestry?"

"Three days ago."

Three days? The shiver increased. "Exactly three days ago I came to the end of my hope and cried out to God for just a word about Tamar."

Veronica gasped. Gilda's eyes overflowed. George nodded. "It happens that way. We had no idea Joy-

Tamar was back in San Francisco. Had she just arrived? If not, why didn't she come to Gilda and me?" Pain showed in the way his face worked.

"We'll never know that until we find her," Gordon said. He glanced out the window into the dark fog. "Tomorrow we'll find her." New confidence rose in him until he wanted to jump and shout. He looked down at the tapestry. "May I keep this?" he asked.

"Of course," Gilda told him.

Veronica spoke for the first time since she had asked about Tamar. "Give it to me and I'll have it cleansed."

Gordon hated to let it go. Somehow, the feeling of Tamar's presence hung about the stained tapestry. Yet if—no, *when* they found her, this symbol must be as bright and lovely as ever. He laid it in Veronica's arms as if it were a casket filled with the richest jewels and gold the world could offer. In her eyes he saw the same gladness that bubbled like a fountain inside him.

The final stretch of the search proved to be anticlimactic. Some intense questioning turned up clues that led to Tamar's bedside. Before Gordon, the Smiths, or even Carlos was allowed in to see her, the doctor had a long talk with them. He eyed each sourly, and Gordon felt accused, tried, and convicted of some heinous crime against the patient.

"She got a mighty whack on the head, pushed herself until others no longer needed her, gave away everything she had. Probably didn't eat or sleep enough to keep a sparrow alive," the doctor bluntly told them. "I've seen them before, these martyrs who forget themselves because others need them. I also suspect something far deeper, an inner conflict that's keeping her disturbed." His brows drew together in a thatch that made a roof over his eyes. "Do any of you know anything about that kind of thing?"

Carlos took it like the man he had become. "It's all my fault." He went on to tell the whole story, with Gordon and the Smiths piecing in the things they knew.

"So none of you actually know where she was or how she got hurt," the doctor summarized.

"I saw her at the Grand Opera House the night before," Gordon confessed. He quickly added, "Forgive me, Carlos. I couldn't tell you when you were thanking God Tamar wasn't here."

The doctor waved it away as irrelevant, leaned back in his chair, and considered. He looked at each in turn. Gordon shifted position in a fever of impatience.

"One thing more. She's called several times for the tapestry. What does she want?"

"This." Gordon brought out the restored tapestry and unfolded it. "A family heirloom."

"I'd like to give this to her before you see her," the doctor said. "Or before she sees you, to be more exact. You may stand to one side but not where she can see you. I'm just not sure how she'd react to any of you."

Gordon's knees were weak when he followed the doctor to a screened-off area. He wondered if he could remain upright. At first the doctor's head blocked his view, but when the gruff old man leaned over, Gordon saw the still figure. Could that be Tamar, shorn until she looked like a beautiful boy, more angelic than human? God, had they come too late? The doctor's forced cheerfulness roused him.

"Tamar, I've brought you your tapestry." He waited then repeated it. The second time a flutter of eyelashes against the pale cheeks sent blood pumping through Gordon's heart. At least she was still alive.

"Open your eyes, Tamar. See?" The doctor held the brightly colored treasure so that when the dark brown eyes opened they focused on it. He gently crumpled it into her hands. A tiny smile crossed Tamar's face and the little gold motes Gordon knew so well danced in her eyes. Then she held the tapestry to her breast, sighed, and dropped back to sleep. Not until she awakened from a long, natural sleep would the doctor permit her to be disturbed and then only after the nurse had fed her broth. At last the nurse said to her, "Someone's here to see you."

Tamar's astonished eyes opened wide. Then the hidden, watching visitors saw fear cloud them. "I-I don't—" Her lips quivered. Her body tensed.

"Mercy sakes, child, you don't have to see anyone but me, if you don't want to." The nurse smoothed her pillow, ran a hand over the cropped hair, and smiled. "Your visitors can just write a note and come another time. All right?"

The rigid figure relaxed and nodded, and the doctor

motioned the others out. "Sorry. This is typical after a blow to the head. Folks get notional. Do what Nurse said. Write her a letter but be all-fired careful what you put in it!"

"May God forgive me for what I've done," Carlos murmured when they gathered outside. "Even if Tamar ever can, I won't be able to forgive myself." Great drops of sweat beaded his face.

Gilda Smith, the simple woman whose faith sustained her in every aspect of life, laid her hand on his arm. "Mr. O'Donnell, God has already forgiven you. So will Tamar. Time will help you put it in the past where it belongs. Now let's do what the doctor suggested and write some cheery letters to our girl."

Still cuddling her tapestry, Tamar slept, roused, drank broth, and slept again. When she awoke, four white envelopes lay on a rude stand beside her. She eyed them several times, then pushed them away. She couldn't, however, push aside the curiosity they roused in her, and the next evening when lamps had been lit to cast a dim glow, she made a decision. In the morning she would read them. The nurse had said they were from a Mr. and Mrs. Smith, a Mr. O'Donnell, a Mr. Rhys, and a Miss Rhys. Her forehead wrinkled. Why would Veronica write and how had they found her? Would Carlos order her to come home? And Gordon—what might his missive contain?

Suddenly she felt feverish. Surely God wouldn't allow her to be tormented further. The dread of what those innocent envelopes housed made her restless, and when the nurse came back to take her temperature, it had risen again.

"What's all this?" she scolded. "Why, you were doing so well we were ready to let you go in a day or two more. Tamar O'Donnell, what's fretting you?"

"The letters. I don't know what they say and I'm afraid."

The nurse laid a cold, wet cloth on the hot face. "My old granny said that when you're afraid of something you should march right up and face it. She insisted that if you do that, whatever it is will almost always just slink away." She lifted the cloth, dipped it, wrung it out, and replaced it. "'Course, sometimes it helps a body if another body's there beside her. D'you want me to open the letters and read them to you? If there's anything worrisome, I'll just take it out and burn it."

"Would you do that, please?" Tamar could scarcely believe the relief that flowed through her. Nurse wouldn't read anything to upset her and good news would help her sleep.

"Which one first?"

"The one from my brother. It's the most likely to hold dynamite." Tamar bundled the tapestry under her chin and prepared to face her worst fears.

twelve

Tamar held her breath while the nurse scanned the few lines of black writing, grunted, and said, "Nothing to fear in this one." She cleared her throat and read.

> *Dear Tamar,*
>   *I have asked God to forgive me. I hope you someday will be able to do the same. I blame myself for your being hurt. All my love,*
> *Carlos.*

Tears of weakness and joy leaked onto the tapestry. The nurse let her cry, then handed her a clean handkerchief. "Blow your nose, child. Which letter shall I read next?"

Tamar couldn't help giggling. "Miss O'Donnell's." Again she waited. Again relief filled her when she heard Veronica's short message expressing thankfulness that Tamar had been found and ending with the sincere wish she would soon be well. An added postscript informed her that Veronica and Gordon had taken a home in Oakland until they decided if they would rebuild, and she hoped Tamar would come to them when the doctor released her.

"Sounds like a fine woman," the nurse approved.

Without being told, she opened the Smith's note, leaving Gordon's for the last. George and Gilda wrote much the same thing as Veronica had, except they added that Gordon had not betrayed Joy to her brother. They also were in the process of getting reestablished, and Gilda ended by saying, "We suspect you won't be needing it, but if you ever want to sing again, our 'Unknown Angel' won't have to look further than the New Pantages Theatre for employment."

"*You* were the Unknown Angel?" the reader exclaimed. "Well, I never! A friend and I heard you sing, and here I've been taking care of you. Wonder if my friend will believe it?"

"You're the one who should be called an angel," Tamar told her, but her gaze strayed to the last letter.

The wise woman hesitated, then said, "So long as you faced up to the first three and none of them leaped up and bit you, seems like maybe you could trust enough to read this one yourself." Her apron swished when she handed Gordon's letter to Tamar. "I'll be back once I've tended to my other patients." She vanished, leaving Tamar to hold the envelope a long time before she dared remove its contents. "Beloved Tamar-Joy," it began. She gasped, felt a rush of hot color to her face, and convulsively crushed the letter in her fingers. The next instant she smoothed the page and read on.

> *Perhaps I should not address you so but much of your trouble has come because I didn't speak*

*sooner. I hesitated due to the short time we had
known each other and had finally made up mind
to tell you how I care just before Carlos arrived
and told me what he had done. I shouted to him
that I loved you and wanted to marry you, then
we raced to the Smiths'. You had gone. You will
never know how I ached, knowing you must feel
I had betrayed you.*

> *We arrived in Oakland and found
Gilda alone by the tracks that took you away.
All our searching proved fruitless. Not until I
glimpsed you at the opera did I know you were
in San Francisco and the look in your eyes
knifed me.*

> *Even if you can never learn to love
me, I thank God you came into my life. During
the terrible times just past, I've learned to rely
on Him with my whole heart. I felt myself
growing old, looking for you among the dead
and dying. No matter if our paths separate, you
will be the woman I love, honor and cherish
until the day I die.*

> *Gordon*

Tamar pressed her lips to the page. Was any woman
so loved as she? To think she had once almost married
Phillip-with-two-l's! Humiliation for even considering it scorched her face.

Yet even happiness could not keep her awake.
Tamar fell asleep with her first love letter lying open

on the richly woven tapestry. The doctor had told her
the part it played in her being found. Now that her
body, mind, and spirit were healing, she dimly remembered a cold child in Layfayette Square, and the
feeling of sacrifice that swept through her when she
gave all she had to the shivering child. To think the
child and his mother later encountered the Smiths!
How good God was to those who loved and served
Him.

Tamar's letters proved to be just the incentive she
needed to get well. From the moment she learned
how loved and cherished she was by her brother, her
friends, and Gordon, the will to live triumphed over
sickness. A week later the Smiths took her to their
rented dwelling place. At her insistence, they chose
a route so she could see the true devastation those
fateful seconds of April eighteenth had wrought.

Rubble and ghastly broken chimneys stood above
charred ruins of buildings. City Hall's statue of
Liberty still stood on its pinnacle, despite the fact the
dome had been torn apart in the quake. Four square
miles of destruction had once been the heart and pride
of San Francisco, but by now, businesses had searched
and found spots from which to resume their daily
tasks. The former quiet residential Van Ness street
bustled with business and professional establishments. Fillmore, that had somehow come through
unharmed, boasted it would one day rival Market
Street. Trolleys again clanged, and the placid Bay
gleamed blue in the sunlight.

Tamar leaned back in the carriage George had bought. "I hope Veronica and—and Gordon weren't hurt when I came with you instead of going to their place." The thought troubled her.

Gilda patted her hand. "I had a little talk with them and they understand."

Tamar gave the soft fingers a little squeeze. "It's just that Carlos said Lorraine would—" She hastily replaced his "have a fit" with "be upset, because of the circumstances."

"The Lorraines of the world have a hard time of it," George observed from the driver's seat.

Tamar's eyes opened wide. "Why, George, what an odd thing to say!"

"Think about it," he advised in his pleasant voice. "All their lives they must do only that which is approved by others of their ilk. Never can they be truly free. Do you know that's why so many people in society have a difficult time accepting salvation?" He went on sadly, "It's a terrible thing to be so prideful you can't or won't bow to anyone, even the Lord Jesus."

Gilda shifted a little on the seat. "Now, George, don't be too critical. You know what happened the Sunday after Easter."

"What did happen?" Tamar asked. "I don't seem to remember."

"Why, child, San Francisco went to church! Not in its usual dress, but garbed in courage and determination. Priests said mass in front of their ruined churches. Ministers preached the gospel of Christ in every square. And the children! They went to Sunday School in Golden Gate Park right next to the beautiful flower beds." She looked wise. "'Twouldn't surprise me but what great good will come out of this whole troubled time."

She cast a roguish glance toward Tamar. "I'd say it already has in some instances." When her companion blushed, Gilda blandly added, "Look at how we found each other again and got misunderstandings straightened out." A shadow darkened her eyes. "If I'd dreamed you weren't on that train and that you misinterpreted Gordon and George arriving with Carlos, I'd never have left the Oakland station." She wiped away a quick tear.

"I just thank God that Joy-Tamar so unselfishly gave away her tapestry to that cold child or we'd be still searching for her," George gruffly said. He guided the horses up an inclined street to a small but charming cottage that overlooked the water. "Well, ladies, we're home."

"What a wonderful word." Tamar noted the cream walls covered with creeping flowers and vines. Once inside, Gilda led her to a room with windows on two sides, a comfortable-looking bed, and sunny yellow curtains that danced a welcome.

"Rest," she said, and helped Tamar out of the old black gown she'd worn when working with the injured. The caring nurse had taken it and washed it, but Gilda frowned. "I hope you'll never wear black again."

Tamar, clad in Gilda's best nightgown, settled wearily into the white-sheeted bed. "I don't have anything else." She pushed herself up straight. "Gilda, take some of the money the nurse put away for me when she found it in my gown and see if you can get me a dress, will you?" She flushed. "Gordon will come soon and I don't want to look ugly."

"Keep your money for other things," Gilda promptly said. "We received our insurance settlement and can well afford to purchase a dress for you." She ignored Tamar's protests, gently pushed her down against the soft pillow, and slipped out. Tamar fell asleep within minutes.

She awakened more rested than she had been in months. Something fluttered in the breeze from the still-open window. "Oh!" Tamar rubbed her eyes and looked again.

"Do you like it?" Gilda asked from the doorway. "I remembered how you looked in the dress you brought from your brother's home and tried to get one just like it."

"It's so lovely," Tamar cried, her gazed fastened on the pale green voile, twin to the one lost in the confusion after the earthquake.

"I'll help you bathe, then why don't you put it on? I picked out a house dress or two, as well, but the Rhyses sent word they would come this evening and you'll want to dress up."

Although Tamar's red-gold hair now curved under

like a page-boy's, the green dress did much toward restoring her self-confidence. Her Spanish-brown eyes warmed when she thought of Gordon seeing her in this dress. Her heart beat rapidly beneath the lacy bodice. Would he speak—tonight?

"If he doesn't, I don't know what I'll do," she confessed to her reflection and turned from the mirror.

Each time the door knocker sounded, Tamar's heart leaped. Yet before Gordon and Veronica called, other visitors arrived. Carlos, a distinctly uncomfortable Lorraine, and—

"Rosa!" Tamar stared at the senorita doll, a beloved relic of her childhood. Scorch stained the doll's fiesta garments, but her dark eyes and hair were intact. Rosa's owner snatched the doll from Carlos's fingers and hugged her. "Oh, where did you find her?"

"That silly maid didn't save a thing of her own," Lorraine sniffed. "But she produced this and said keeping the doll was keeping a promise."

"She couldn't rescue your books," Carlos put in.

"It doesn't matter." Tamar still clutched the doll. "I'm just so glad we're all safe."

Lorraine's chin went into the air and her gray-green eyes chilled. "Oh, safe, but we lost everything." The corners of her mouth tilted down. "Carlos says we'll rebuild but I wonder if it's worth it."

"I understand the best Nob Hill families do plan to stay and rebuild," Gilda said guilelessly.

Lorraine brightened and permitted herself the lux-

ury of a smile. "In that case we probably will, too."
She went into a rambling list of what she wanted in
her new home until Tamar wanted to scream. Why
didn't they go? Veronica and Gordon were due any
moment. How awful for them to have to meet and
endure this social-climbing woman!

Jesus loves and died for her.

Tamar started. The whispered reminder in her soul
softened her spirit toward her tiresome sister-in-law.
Even when the Rhyses arrived and Lorraine babbled
on and on, Tamar clung to the thought; she only
smiled at the older woman's prying comments. Perhaps Carlos sensed his sister's turmoil, however, for
he told Lorraine they must go and hurried her away
despite her protests.

With her fine ability to smooth situations, Veronica
asked, "Would you show me your new home?" She
and the Smiths left Tamar and Gordon alone in the
room.

Tamar lifted her face to the breeze that blew through
the open window, and smelled the cool scent of the
Bay; she could not make herself look at Gordon, even
when he took a chair and placed it next to her own.
"How are you feeling?" he asked her.

Trying to control her emotions, she glanced around
the inviting room. "How could anyone help getting
well in such a cozy, welcoming home?"

"Is this the kind of home you want, someday?"

Disappointment surged through her. He sounded
so formal, so lacking in feeling, she could scarcely

believe he had ever written to her of love. And his words implied only a polite interest in her future.

"I can imagine nothing better," she replied. "As you know, I've lived in several different houses—but this one is furnished with love." A wistful note crept into her voice.

Gordon abruptly rose. Her heart sank. Surely he wasn't leaving! Instead he crossed to the couch, knelt beside it, and looked deep into her eyes.

"I sent you a letter."

"Yes." Her lips trembled. She clasped her fingers tightly and looked down at them.

"Tamar, I meant every word of it. I love you more than anything except my Lord. Can you ever learn to care for me?"

"I-I already do."

He leaned closer, as if doubting his ears. "Beloved, will you please say it again?"

She raised her head. Tears of joy and weakness fell. "I love you, Gordon—more than anything next to my Lord."

He took her hands and his gray eyes warmed to the softness of San Francisco fog. "You will be my wife?"

"Yes." She pushed herself up and swayed toward him. Their first kiss held the promise of greater earthly happiness than she had ever thought possible. Gordon held her close, and she felt his heart marking time with her own until voices and footsteps warned that the others were returning. Before they did, Gordon slipped a ring on the third finger of her left hand and whispered, "It reminded me of you."

She only had a moment to glimpse the blazing gold topaz set in tiny sparkling diamonds before he slipped back to his chair.

"You haven't tired her, have you?" Veronica demanded.

"Oh, no!"

Tamar automatically held out her hands in a wave of protest, then turned rosy when George Smith observed, "Folks don't get tired when they're in love."

The new fiancee saw the exchange of glances between him and Gilda. Tamar smiled; like the Smiths, she and Gordon would experience the deepening love that came with years together serving God and one another. How blessed she was and how incredible it seemed that just a few short months ago she'd wondered why God didn't appear to care if she ever again knew happiness.

"When will you be married?" Veronica asked as she embraced Tamar.

"Give a fellow time, will you?" Gordon pleaded. "I just got the ring on her finger and here you're worried when the wedding's going to be. Naturally, I hope it's soon but that's up to my bride-to-be."

His look brought even more color to Tamar's face. "Why, I—"

"Child, you don't have to decide right now," George put in. His round face beamed. "One thing, you're not fit right now for all the stress of a big wedding. Why don't you just stay with Gilda and me for a time?"

"That's a good idea," Gordon admitted, although disappointment lurked in his eyes. "Veronica, we've outstayed ourselves and I do have work that must be done tonight, betrothal or not." They left in a flood of laughter.

"I'll need to tell Carlos—and Lorraine—soon." A little of Tamar's contentment fled.

Gilda quietly told her, "You may wish to have your plans all made with Gordon before you announce your engagement. Sometimes it's best to be prepared, although I believe your sister-in-law will fall in line with what the Rhyses want."

"That's probably best," Tamar agreed. "Could we be married right here, with just Carlos and Lorraine, Veronica, and my brother Dick? It's so homey and . . . ." Her voice trailed off.

"We will be honored if that's what you choose," George said huskily. He came to the couch, pumped her hand up and down, and reminded, "You couldn't marry a finer man than Gordon Rhys. He will do what you wish, I'm sure."

Gordon readily agreed to Tamar's request with one stipulation; Hood must be included in the small guest list. He had worked hard keeping track of Tamar and would feel snubbed to be omitted. Together with Veronica, whose help they enlisted in handling Lorraine, they approached the O'Donnells.

"Why the idea," Lorraine immediately protested. "A hole-in-the-corner wedding for an O'Donnell?"

Gordon and Tamar sent looks of dismay at her but Veronica came through beautifully. "You know, an ostentatious wedding right now might be interpreted wrong." She shrugged her square shoulders. "You understand, Mrs. O'Donnell. With San Francisco busy rebuilding and all, we are forced to forfeit some of the little niceties."

Lorraine did a complete about-face. "You are so right, Miss Rhys. For a moment I forgot the circumstances." She turned back to Gordon and ignored Tamar. "What date have you set?"

Mischief filled his face and his eyes sparkled. "We thought of October tenth. That gives us several months to select a home or have one constructed and I can take a month off in the fall for a honeymoon."

"October tenth!" Lorraine's face mottled. "But that's—"

"—just the right date," Carlos interrupted, with a look that quelled his overbearing wife.

"One thing," Gordon began hesitantly. "We'd like to have Dick live with us."

"But he's going to West Point as soon as he's old enough." Lorraine's eyes flashed dangerously and Tamar braced herself. "Until then, he will remain in the school my husband selected."

"There's been a change in plans," Carlos informed her. Not a wink of his eyelash gave away the long session in Gordon's office where Carlos had learned many things about his younger brother, especially how he hated all things military and longed to have a real home. Gordon had taken pains to go see Dick and win the boy's confidence. "Dick has shown an interest in law and Gordon has graciously consented to let him work in the office this summer. There are plenty of good schools right here in San Francisco and should Dick stick with wanting to become an attorney, he can get no better training than from Gordon."

Tamar's eyes flooded. Neither Gordon nor Carlos had told her of the plan. Oh, to be with Dick again! To see his dear face and snapping black eyes. Gratitude welled up within her, so much she didn't even care to laugh when Veronica approved the idea and Lorraine endorsed it as if it had been her own.

"I still don't see why you're waiting so long to get married," the blonde woman fretted.

"We haven't had much of a courtship." Gordon smiled at Tamar. "Now we will, even though this will be a summer of hard work."

thirteen

A few days later George opened a newspaper and began to laugh. "Young lady, you have made the news."

"I?" Tamar lifted amazed eyebrows. "What have I done?"

George chuckled until his plump body shook. "Listen to this. I suspect it's your sister-in-law's doing." He began to read.

> Mr. and Mrs. Carlos O'Donnell announce the betrothal of his sister, Tamar Joy O'Donnell, to Gordon Rhys, noted San Francisco attorney-at-law. Out of loyalty to a city engrossed in rebuilding, the formal wedding expected of such an eminent couple will be sacrificed. A private wedding is scheduled for sometime in October.
>
> Mr. Rhys is busily engaged in civic affairs and by serving on several prominent committees with Mr. O'Donnell, has been instrumental in helping to bring order out of chaos. Miss O'Donnell's lovely voice captured the hearts of San Franciscans when she sang for a limited time at the Pantages Theatre. It is doubtful

whether Miss O'Donnell, or the Unknown Angel as she was called by the finest critics, will be singing in public again, due to illness after her heroic efforts in the aftermath of the earthquake and fire.

In an exclusive interview with Mrs. Carlos O'Donnell, she refused to disclose the many selfless acts of her beloved sister-in-law and merely stated, "Tamar wants no publicity or thanks for all she did, but then, true angels of mercy seldom do."

Congratulations are in order to Gordon Rhys for winning such a charming young lady. Our city is blessed indeed to have both of these worthy citizens plus the O'Donnells and Miss Veronica Rhys as residents.

"How appalling!" Tamar's face burned with disgust. "This is even lower than I thought Lorraine would stoop." She took the paper from George, scanned it, and indignantly repeated, "Sacrifice a public wedding? We sound like martyrs."

"I liked the part about the angel of mercy," George said. "I'd sure like to hear about all those undisclosed selfless acts, Joy-Tamar."

"So would I," the tormented bride-to-be muttered.

"Laugh if off, child." Gilda's wide smile soothed her. "If that's the only way the poor woman can be happy, let her alone." She sighed. "If she only knew of her Father's love, she wouldn't have to seek fame elsewhere."

The words sank deep into Tamar's troubled mind. All during the spring and summer months while Gordon toiled and she regained her health, she thought about Lorraine, until one day she told Gilda. "I have to speak to her about salvation and I'd rather face a storm in the ocean."

"Have you been putting it off?"

"Yes. I can't much longer, especially now." The latest edition of the papers had carried a splashy story about the recently disclosed criminal activity of Phillip-with-two-l's. The reporter had spiced up the story of Carlin's arrest by reminding the readers that Phillip had been left waiting at the church the previous fall by Miss Tamar O'Donnell who would soon wed Gordon Rhys. The account ended with an editorial-type comment, "It appears Miss O'Donnell knew what she was about when she failed to appear at the church."

"Let's have a word of prayer," Gilda suggested. Kneeling between her friends, Tamar felt support for the unpleasant task before her. Still, her stomach fluttered as she made the short trip to Lorraine and Carlos's temporary home. Would her sister-in-law be humbled by the newspaper story, or would she be in tears, furious? Could this be God's way of softening the hard-caked earth of her heart so the seed of salvation could be planted and grow?

With her usual unpredictableness, Lorraine distorted history to her own choosing. "Well, Tamar, I always told you not to encourage Phillip Carlin." Her every hair was in perfect order, but her white skin was mottled. "Why you ever let things get as far as you did, I'll never know. All he wanted was the inheritance he thought you'd have."

Speechless, Tamar fell into a chair.

Lorraine ranted on. "To think that your name is being bandied on the lips of the commonest persons in the city!" She shuddered delicately and sighed the sigh of the persecuted. "Of course, it never occurred to you that association with such a scoundrel would reflect on the rest of us. I'm just thankful that the Rhyses are so forgiving." Her eyes glittered, daring Tamar to defend herself.

Suddenly Tamar stood, crossed to Lorraine, and put her arms around her. It felt like embracing a poker. Then the slim body relaxed and Tamar whispered, "Lorraine, I never had a sister. Won't you be one? I need you, so much."

Could that be a sob? Lorraine's arms crept about the younger woman and she brokenly said, "No one has ever told me that." She held Tamar away from her. "Carlos is so self-sufficient and no children came."

Enlightenment filled Tamar. It emboldened her to say, "There is One who loves you more than life itself, One who chose you as His own, created you and made you unique. Lorraine, our Heavenly Father loved you so much He sent His only Son that you could be saved and live with Him forever."

"I know." Lorraine bit her lip and tears gushed.

"Then why don't you invite Him into your heart?" Tamar asked.

For a moment she thought the Holy Spirit had won. Then Lorraine stepped back. A mask slid over her face. "When God shows He really loves me and sends me the son Carlos wants so badly, I'll accept Christ."

"Oh, Lorraine, don't try to bargain with God," Tamar cried. "I know what it's like, saying if You do this, I'll do that. It doesn't work. It never will! God doesn't want us to become His children simply because we're grateful for something He's given us— unless it's gratitude for Jesus." She held her breath.

Lorraine's voice warmed; perhaps the ice that had encased her for so long was beginning to melt. "I do want you to love me." It was the closest to an apology for the past Tamar knew she would ever get. "I'll think about the other." With a return to her normal air, she straightened. "Now, let's speak no more of— things."

Tamar leaned forward. "Please, talk over what I said with Carlos. Ever since the earthquake, I have the feeling he has grown closer to God than at any time in his life."

"Yes. And farther from me." Lorraine clamped her lips shut.

A few moments later Tamar excused herself, but all the way back to the Smiths', she pondered in her heart the unsuspected depths of the woman she once hated and feared. She bowed her head and prayed for Lorraine.

Meanwhile, Dick O'Donnell had bounced back into Tamar's life with all the enthusiasm of a sixteen-year-old set free from drudgery. Gordon had invited the boy to live with him and Veronica until the fall wedding, but he chose to stay in the Smiths' spare room. His snapping dark eyes and cheerful whistle filled the quiet home with life. For the first time, he learned all the details of Tamar's adventurous months since she slid down her bed sheet rope.

"You're one brave sister," he approved. Then his face darkened and he clenched his fists. "If I ever get my hands on that Carlin, he will wish he'd never heard the name O'Donnell."

"Phillip-with-two-l's won't be around for some time," George Smith told him. "Rumor has it this time he's caught for good. Something about selling worthless stock in a rebuilding firm that only exists in his mind."

Tamar could only feel relief. Even though months had passed since her would-be-husband turned up at the Gregories' musicale in Oakland, she couldn't forget the moment of desperation when he demanded her precious tapestry as the price for his silence.

She shoved the memory aside and concentrated on preparing for her marriage with Gordon. True to his word, he spent every free moment with her, courting her as he had promised. She learned the simple joy of being with him. Sometimes they sought a quiet place in Golden Gate Park just before sundown. Several times on a Saturday she tiptoed from her room, met him at the door, and they watched the sun rise over the recovering city. She never failed to feel humble that of all the eligible women in San Francisco he had chosen her.

"You sure picked a winner," Dick heartily approved, then hesitated. The Smiths had gone to check on the progress of the New Pantages, and Dick and Tamar had the house to themselves. "Uh, you're sure I'm not going to be in the way? After all, most newlyweds don't want a brother hanging around." He laughed anxiously.

"Dick, dear, Gordon would never have suggested it if he didn't want you," Tamar reassured.

"Good." He dropped the subject, although relief shone in his eyes. "Hey, Gilda told me you've agreed to sing once more before you get married, for some kind of children's relief fund."

She smiled at him, loving his presence after their long time apart. Bees hummed in the flowers around them, and brightly colored birds darted and sang. Could anything be more peaceful? "Yes." She gazed at the whitecaps playing tag on the Bay. "Pray for good weather. It's to be in the New Pantages Theatre but the roof isn't on yet. Volunteers are trucking in chairs, though, and the sponsors have commandeered some of the best talent they can get on short notice."

"Including the Unknown Angel. Are you going to masquerade as her again?" Dick hunched forward, eyes alight with interest.

Tamar's laugh rippled out. "It isn't necessary now

that everyone knows me. I'm going to wear a new white gown and George suggested that we drape my tapestry over a screen for a background. They'll run pictures in the papers of some of us who will perform."

A strange shiver touched her in spite of the warm afternoon. She wondered why. Surely she didn't fear performing. As before, she'd sing three times, ending with the triumphant hymn, "O God, Our Help in Ages Past." The magnificent words of encouragement signified San Francisco's struggle to survive and would remind the audience of their sole protection against storm and trouble. If only some would heed and accept that message.

Captioned "The Unknown Angel Sings Again," the newspaper write-up created a stir in the middle of the hard task of restoration. Donald and Dora Wilson, who had cried for days after their beloved Joy left, clamored to go when Cook proudly showed them the picture. Their fluffy little mother boasted to anyone who would listen that, "I suspected all along poor Miss O'Donnell was incognito," before wistfully adding, "And she was also the best children's companion we ever had!"

"And she would have stayed with us a lot longer if your idiot brother Edgar had left her alone," her husband sarcastically observed. "I just hope to heaven that lawyer she's marrying never decides to look Edgar up."

In Oakland, Mrs. Gregory pouted over her lost

chance to sponsor the singer who had turned out to be one of *the* O'Donnells, but Alice just sighed. No music teacher since Miss Darnell had ever been so kind or pretty.

An unknown mother who saw and recognized the tapestry penned a tear-stained note of thanks for once having it wrapped around her cold child.

And Phillip-with-two-l's, who had managed to escape the law and hide in an obscure corner until he could flee the city, clutched the paper with greedy fingers. A glint turned his hazel eyes to ugly slits. So. Tamar, who had caused all his trouble by leaving him humiliated at the church, still possessed the tapestry. A slow smile crossed his hardened face. If he could get that tapestry and slip away, its selling price would keep him for some time. He immediately dyed his hair, purchased a muffler to cover the lower part of his face, and hurried to buy a ticket for the concert, painfully aware of his dwindling supply of funds. The short time between the announcement and the event gave him time to fan the fire of his accusations. "She deserves what she gets," he told himself a dozen times. "I'd never have resorted to fraud if Tamar hadn't forced me into it." His grip on reason faded until all he could see was the tapestry, offering hope and salvation from the misery of being wanted by the law.

Perhaps even Caruso wouldn't have been more enthusiastically greeted than those who gave of their talents at the benefit. Act followed act. Applause rose and fell. Light and laughter and release from cares combined into a joyous experience. After the seats had been filled, crowds stood in the streets. Good-natured policemen lingered among them to hear. Tamar's wish for good weather came true and a million stars shone down on the roofless New Pantages.

"Our final performance is by Miss Tamar Joy O'Donnell," George Smith announced. "Formerly called the Unknown Angel." A burst of cheering interrupted any further tribute and Gilda took her place at the piano. The lights had been turned out between acts and when they came on, Tamar stood straight and lovely, gowned in white, with the scarlet and emerald and white tapestry as a backdrop. No mantilla hid her hair or face, but a red rose nestled in the lace at her throat, its twin in her red-gold hair. The haunting notes of "Greensleeves" filled the theater and spilled out the open doors into the evening. A storm of applause made her pause for a long time before Gilda began playing a rollicking gypsy song. Again she stood waiting until the audience quieted. Then putting her whole heart into the music, she sang,

"O God, our help in ages past,
Our hope for years to come,
Our shelter from the stormy blast,
And our eternal home!"

Carlos grasped Lorraine's carefully manicured hand

and looked at her. A look unlike any he'd seen since their marriage stole across her face, and she squeezed her husband's hand.

Gordon Rhys felt the power of the Holy Spirit working through the woman he loved, and tears blurred the white figure standing with outstretched arms. When the audience surged to its feet on the last verse and spontaneously joined in, Gordon couldn't sing the final words,

> "Be thou our guard while troubles last
> And our eternal home."

God, help many to accept Your Son, Gordon silently prayed as the crowd raised their voices in tribute to singer and song.

At last the stage lights went out, the curtain fell before rising again with the entire cast. A minute passed. Two. People called, "Bring them out!" But when the curtain lifted, the cast milled about a fallen white figure.

"Tamar!" Gordon plowed through the babbling crowd and vaulted to the stage with Dick close behind, then Carlos.

"She's all right, sir, but he—a man, when the lights dimmed, he pushed her aside, snatched the tapestry from behind her and shot off the stage," someone cried.

"Stay with her. I'll go." Dick made a flying leap in the direction the thief had taken. He burst out the stage door and careened into two policemen. "Quick, did anyone come out?"

"No." They sprang to attention. "Is there trouble?"

"A thief," Dick explained briefly and dashed back inside. Was that a darker shadow at the end of an unlit hall? He pelted toward it. Saw it move. "Stop, thief!" Dick put on speed, launched himself like a cannon-ball, and felled the man who struggled to no avail against the boy's healthy young strength.

"You can let him up," a grim voice ordered, and Dick sprang off the still-kicking man. A policeman yanked the thief to his feet. Carlos came running from backstage, and the man squirmed again.

"I've done nothing! Let me go," he shouted furiously.

"He stole this priceless tapestry from my sister Tamar O'Donnell," Dick yelled and grabbed it from behind the man.

"Who are you, anyway?" The policeman demanded. He grabbed the man's chin and raised it. "Say, you're the guy who broke out of jail last night. Carlin. That's it. I oughta get a promotion outa this." He snapped handcuffs on Carlin, who still protested he had only picked up the tapestry.

"Wish I'd known sooner who he was," Dick lamented when the policeman and his partner hustled Phillip off. "I'd have given him a few licks he wouldn't forget!" He tossed the tousled hair out of his eyes. "Tamar's all right, isn't she?"

"She's fine." Carlos passed one hand in front of his

eyes and color stole back to his ghastly face. "Let's get this to her." He motioned toward the tapestry. "Dick—thanks."

" 'Sall right." His brother grinned and flexed his muscles, but when they reached Tamar he dropped to his knees beside Gordon, who had pulled her into his arms regardless of onlookers. "Here's your rug. Kind of crumpled but it's not torn or anything. Carlin stole it."

Tamar laughed until she cried. "Phillip-with-two-l's. I didn't think he had it in him." She laughed again and demanded that Gordon set her on her feet. "Tell them everything is all right," she implored after a lightning glance at the concerned crowd. "No, there's a better way. Carlos, ask Gilda to start playing 'The Star Spangled Banner.'" Flanked by her brothers, she made room for Gordon and Lorraine, and then Tamar led the house in song.

Finally people dispersed. So did the cast members. At last only the Smiths, O'Donnells, and Gordon remained.

"Tamar, I can't stand to wait until October for us to be married," Gordon burst out. "After this, I'll never be happy until you are my wife. Will you marry me next week? Hood can keep things going for a time."

Tamar looked into his eyes. Her fingers held the tapestry that had been taken from her, retrieved; given away, found; stolen, returned. The Master Weaver had allowed dark threads to wind their way into her life, but they only enhanced the brightness of what lay

ahead: life with Gordon, followed by eternal life with
the Weaver. She nodded and held out her hands. The
tapestry covered them, spilling its warmth over their
love. She glanced around the close-knit little circle.
Carlos and Lorraine stood with arms around each
other. A new softness showed on Lorraine's face.
George and Gilda had clasped hands. Dick's feet
were apart, his arms crossed.

*Please, God, make our lives beautiful for You and
one day save us all,* Tamar silently prayed. She freed
her hands, draped the tapestry over her shoulders
serape-style, and threw her head back for a last look
at the stars.

Long after the unfinished theater lay empty, long
after Tamar slept, the essence of a mighty prayer
lingered over the hills of San Francisco:

> Be thou our guard while troubles last
> And our eternal home.

Tomorrow beckoned, with its joys and uncertain-
ties. Tonight, the pulse of a city had been quickened
by the promise of salvation.

A Letter To Our Readers

Dear Reader:

In order that we might better contribute to your reading enjoyment, we would appreciate your taking a few minutes to respond to the following questions. When completed, please return to the following:

Karen Carroll, Editor
Heartsong Presents
P.O. Box 719
Uhrichsville, Ohio 44683

1. Did you enjoy reading *Tapestry of Tamar*?
   ☐ Very much. I would like to see more books by this author!
   ☐ Moderately
   I would have enjoyed it more if _____

   _____

2. Are you a member of *Heartsong Presents*? Yes   No
   If no, where did you purchase this book? _____

   _____

3. What influenced your decision to purchase this book? (Circle those that apply.)

Cover	Back cover copy
Title	Friends
Publicity	Other _____

4. On a scale from 1 (poor) to 10 (superior), please rate the following elements.

    ___Heroine   ___Plot

    ___Hero   ___Inspirational theme

    ___Setting   ___Secondary characters

5. What settings would you like to see covered in *Heartsong Presents* books?

    _____

    _____

6. What are some inspirational themes you would like to see treated in future books?_____

    _____

    _____

7. Would you be interested in reading other *Heartsong Presents* titles?   Yes   No

8. Please circle your age range:

Under 18	18-24	25-34
35-45	46-55	Over 55

9. How many hours per week do you read? _____

Name _____

Occupation _____

Address _____

City _____ State _____ Zip _____

...... Hearts❤ng ......

Great Inspirational Romance at a Great Price!

Heartsong Presents books are inspirational romances in contemporary and historical settings, designed to give you an enjoyable, spirit-lifting reading experience. You can choose from 52 wonderfully written titles from some of today's best authors like Collen Reece, Jacquelyn Cook, Yvonne Lehman, and many others.

HEARTSONG PRESENTS TITLES AVAILABLE NOW:

___HP 1 A TORCH FOR TRINITY, *Colleen L. Reece*
___HP 2 WILDFLOWER HARVEST, *Colleen L. Reece*
___HP 3 RESTORE THE JOY, *Sara Mitchell*
___HP 4 REFLECTIONS OF THE HEART, *Sally Laity*
___HP 5 THIS TREMBLING CUP, *Marlene Chase*
___HP 6 THE OTHER SIDE OF SILENCE, *Marlene Chase*
___HP 7 CANDLESHINE, *Colleen L. Reece*
___HP 8 DESERT ROSE, *Colleen L. Reece*
___HP 9 HEARTSTRINGS, *Irene B. Brand*
___HP10 SONG OF LAUGHTER, *Lauraine Snelling*
___HP11 RIVER OF FIRE, *Jacquelyn Cook*
___HP12 COTTONWOOD DREAMS, *Norene Morris*
___HP13 PASSAGE OF THE HEART, *Kjersti Hoff Baez*
___HP14 A MATTER OF CHOICE, *Susannah Hayden*
___HP15 WHISPERS ON THE WIND, *Maryn Langer*
___HP16 SILENCE IN THE SAGE, *Colleen L. Reece*
___HP17 LLAMA LADY, *VeraLee Wiggins*
___HP18 ESCORT HOMEWARD, *Eileen M. Berger*
___HP19 A PLACE TO BELONG, *Janelle Jamison*
___HP20 SHORES OF PROMISE, *Kate Blackwell*
___HP21 GENTLE PERSUASION, *Veda Boyd Jones*
___HP22 INDY GIRL, *Brenda Bancroft*
___HP23 GONE WEST, *Kathleen Karr*
___HP24 WHISPERS IN THE WILDERNESS, *Colleen L. Reece*
___HP25 REBAR, *Mary Carpenter Reid*
___HP26 MOUNTAIN HOUSE, *Mary Louise Colln*
___HP27 BEYOND THE SEARCHING RIVER, *Jacquelyn Cook*
___HP28 DAKOTA DAWN, *Lauraine Snelling*

(If ordering from this page, please remember to include it with the order form.)

·········Presents·········

_____HP29 FROM THE HEART, *Sara Mitchell*
_____HP30 A LOVE MEANT TO BE, *Brenda Bancroft*
_____HP31 DREAM SPINNER, *Sally Laity*
_____HP32 THE PROMISED LAND, *Kathleen Karr*
_____HP33 SWEET SHELTER, *VeraLee Wiggins*
_____HP34 UNDER A TEXAS SKY, *Veda Boyd Jones*
_____HP35 WHEN COMES THE DAWN, *Brenda Bancroft*
_____HP36 THE SURE PROMISE, *JoAnn A. Grote*
_____HP37 DRUMS OF SHELOMOH, *Yvonne Lehman*
_____HP38 A PLACE TO CALL HOME, *Eileen M. Berger*
_____HP39 RAINBOW HARVEST, *Norene Morris*
_____HP40 PERFECT LOVE, *Janelle Jamison*
_____HP41 FIELDS OF SWEET CONTENT, *Norma Jean Lutz*
_____HP42 SEARCH FOR TOMORROW, *Mary Hawkins*
_____HP43 VEILED JOY, *Colleen L. Reece*
_____HP44 DAKOTA DREAM, *Lauraine Snelling*
_____HP45 DESIGN FOR LOVE, *Janet Gortsema*
_____HP46 THE GOVERNOR'S DAUGHTER, *Veda Boyd Jones*
_____HP47 TENDER JOURNEYS, *Janelle Jamison*
_____HP48 SHORES OF DELIVERANCE, *Kate Blackwell*
_____HP49 YESTERDAY'S TOMORROWS, *Linda Herring*
_____HP50 DANCE IN THE DISTANCE, *Kjersti Hoff Baez*
_____HP51 THE UNFOLDING HEART, *JoAnn A. Grote*
_____HP52 TAPESTRY OF TAMAR, *Colleen L. Reece*

ABOVE TITLES ARE $2.95 EACH

SEND TO: Heartsong Presents Reader's Service
P.O. Box 719, Uhrichsville, Ohio 44683

Please send me the items checked above. I am enclosing $ _____
(please add $1.00 to cover postage per order). Send check or
money order, no cash or C.O.D.s, please.
   To place a credit card order, call **1-800-847-8270.**

NAME _____

ADDRESS _____

CITY/STATE _____ ZIP_____

LOVE A GREAT LOVE STORY?

Introducing Heartsong Presents —
Your Inspirational Book Club

Heartsong Presents Christian romance reader's service will provide you with four never before published romance titles every month! In fact, your books will be mailed to you at the same time advance copies are sent to book reviewers. You'll preview each of these new and unabridged books before they are released to the general public.

These books are filled with the kind of stories you have been longing for—stories of courtship, chivalry, honor, and virtue. Strong characters and riveting plot lines will make you want to read on and on. Romance is not dead, and each of these romantic tales will remind you that Christian faith is still the vital ingredient in an intimate relationship filled with true love and honest devotion.

Sign up today to receive your first set. Send no money now. We'll bill you only $9.97 post-paid with your shipment. Then every month you'll automatically receive the latest four "hot off the press" titles for the same low post-paid price of $9.97. That's a savings of 50% off the $4.95 cover price. When you consider the exaggerated shipping charges of other book clubs, your savings are even greater!

THERE IS NO RISK—you may cancel at any time without obligation. And if you aren't completely satisfied with any selection, return it for an immediate refund.

TO JOIN, just complete the coupon below, mail it today, and get ready for hours of wholesome entertainment.

Now you can curl up, relax, and enjoy some great reading full of the warmhearted spirit of romance.